"You just don't quit, do you?" January said with exasperation.

"No. I don't quit," Michael said, stopping the car and turning off the motor. "Not when I'm going after something I really want."

An awareness flared in her eyes that even the twilight couldn't hide. "There must be a hundred more marketable topics you could write about."

"I'm not talking about an article anymore." He leaned over and unfastened her seat belt. "I want to see you, January. You fascinate me."

She sucked in a sharp breath. "I frustrate you," she corrected him. "You're just not used to being told no."

He cupped her jaw in his hand and slowly turned her face toward him. "What I'm not used to is being turned inside out by the sound of one woman's voice, by the thought of how that woman's mouth would feel against mine." His gaze dropped to her mouth and lingered. When her tongue unconsciously slipped between her lips to wet them, he nearly exploded. "Do you think about that too, January? Do you think what it would be like with me?"

She seemed to wilt, to go all soft and yearning. Then she swallowed hard and met his gaze with a fire in her eyes that even the pouring rain wouldn't have doused. "You're out of line."

"Sorry, January, I really wanted to take this slow, but—" He paused, then forged ahead. "I want to kiss you, January. Would you let me?"

WHAT ARE *LOVESWEPT* ROMANCES?

They are stories of true romance and touching emotion. We believe those two very important ingredients are constants in our highly sensual and very believable stories in the *LOVESWEPT* line. Our goal is to give you, the reader, stories of consistently high quality that may sometimes make you laugh, sometimes make you cry, but are always fresh and creative and contain many delightful surprises within their pages.

Most romance fans read an enormous number of books. Those they truly love, they keep. Others may be traded with friends and soon forgotten. We hope that each *LOVESWEPT* romance will be a treasure—a "keeper." We will always try to publish

LOVE STORIES YOU'LL NEVER FORGET
BY AUTHORS YOU'LL ALWAYS REMEMBER

The Editors

Cindy Gerard

Temptation from the Past

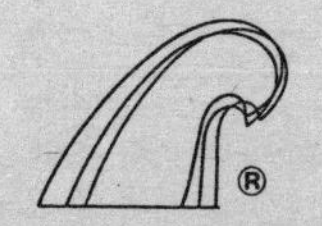

BANTAM BOOKS
NEW YORK • TORONTO • LONDON • SYDNEY • AUCKLAND

TEMPTATION FROM THE PAST

A Bantam Book / December 1991

ISBN 0-553-44174-4

Published simultaneously in the United States and Canada

Bantam Books are published by Bantam Books, a division of Bantam Doubleday Dell Publishing Group, Inc. Its trademark, consisting of the words "Bantam Books" and the portrayal of a rooster, is Registered in U.S. Patent and Trademark Office and in other countries. Marca Registrada. Bantam Books, 666 Fifth Avenue, New York, New York 10103.

PRINTED IN THE UNITED STATES OF AMERICA

OPM 0 9 8 7 6 5 4 3 2 1

Dedication

For my heroes, Tom and Kyle
And of course, George

One

"You know what you really need, don't you?"

Sighing patiently, January Stewart removed her reading glasses. She glanced up from the brief she was finishing into the sparkling though faded hazel eyes of her sixty-five-year-old secretary, Helen Morgan. "I don't need a lecture, if that's what you had in mind," she said with gentle admonishment.

Ignoring the warning, Helen said decisively, "You need to get laid."

January grinned in spite of herself. Everything about Helen was outrageous, from her blue shine-in-the-dark eye shadow and Cupid's-bow red lips to her flaming orange hair. Each shocking, ridiculous quirk was part and parcel of why January for five years had fought daily impulses either to hug Helen or fire her.

Since hugging was something she'd never learned to do gracefully, and since Helen would never stand for being fired, January just shook her head. "Getting laid, as you so delicately put it, is your answer for everything since you met Leonard."

"Hey," Helen said with a smug grin, "it works for

me, sweetie, and until you come up with a better solution, you won't find this kid trying to fix something that ain't broke. A man, my dear, can do wonders for one's . . ." She paused for effect, then finished with a wicked smile. ". . . attitude. Besides, some good sex might cut some of the tension that's putting the dark circles under your sweet little cocoa brown eyes."

Since being widowed ten years earlier and finally finding love again last May with Leonard Tyler, Helen had been driving January crazy with her insistence that a man could cure everything from anxiety to tooth decay.

Extending the dozen or so pages of notes she'd compiled on the Garner case, January graced Helen with a benign yet dismissive smile. "I need this dictation for court tomorrow."

Helen rose regally from her chair, tugged her paisley vest over a waistline that had never been trim, and tucked the dictation under her arm. "Fine," she said in that high, tight voice she reserved for when things were not fine. "Play it your way. But just remember what happened to Jack."

"Jack?" January slipped her glasses back into place.

"You remember. . . . All work and no play Jack?"

"Oh, that Jack. Not to worry, Helen. I'm already as dull as a rubber knife, and I seriously doubt that I'll turn into a boy at this stage in my life."

"At this stage in your life," Helen added with a glare meant to remind January that her twenty-eighth birthday had come and gone the previous month without so much as a dinner date, "you should have a lusty husband messing up you and your bed, and a couple of apple-cheeked babies warming your cold, workaholic heart."

"Workaholics make lousy marriage partners. Consider I'm doing my bid to keep the rising divorce rate in check."

Helen grunted. "You've got more excuses to avoid a relationship than Leonard has plaid pants. *What* are you afraid of? For the life of me, I do not understand you. Why don't you take advantage of that face and tall, lean body of yours, and wear something other than those sedate navy suits and those prissy white blouses that hide your pretty assets? Contacts would be great, and you could cut and curl your hair," she added, really getting into it.

"I don't want contacts, and there's nothing wrong with my hair."

"You could be having such a good time," Helen went on as if she hadn't heard January. "That sexy Lance O'Brian has been calling for you again. Why won't you give him or one of the other attorneys from city hall a tumble? Why, one teacupful of encouragement from you and you could—"

"Get myself laid?" January interrupted drolly. "At the risk of missing out on what promises to be a really meaningful relationship, I'll pass, thank you."

"You're right," Helen said after a lengthy pause. "You really are a deadly dull person, Jan."

"I am a busy person . . . and so should you be." She slanted a pointed glance at the dictation.

With a "humph" and a swirl of rose-colored silk, Helen headed for the door on her four-inch stiletto heels, leaving behind the lingering scent of her exotic, sultry perfume.

January watched Helen settle in behind her word processor, fighting the urge to close the floor-to-ceiling miniblinds that covered the glass wall that separated her office from the reception area. But if she closed the blinds, Helen would know for certain she was hiding something. Then again, what was the point? Helen always knew when something was wrong.

And blast it all, there *was* something bothering her.

January slumped back in her chair. Fiddling absently with a pen, she stared out the street-level window. Not until the noise of a rusted-out cab with its muffler skidding along the cracked pavement slashed through the quiet did January realize with disgust that she was doing it again, tuning out. She didn't have time for this nonsense. Yet for over six months now, January "The Ice Princess" Stewart had found herself feeling the low, dull ache of loneliness. At the oddest moments she'd catch herself wondering—no, worse, *wanting*—to experience what Helen experienced with Leonard. To know what all the fuss was about when things were good between a woman and a man.

Since she didn't have the slightest hint of what to do about it, January did what she always did to combat what she considered a weakness. She turned back to the file on her desk and buried herself in her work. She'd convinced Judge Stone to hold the record on the Garner case open until she'd had time to prepare a brief. He'd extended that time until tomorrow, and for the Garner child's sake she'd better be ready.

Two hours later, as she scanned the case record one last time, she was barely aware of the roar of a motorcycle coming to a halt outside her window. Helen's laughter soon brought her attention to the outer office.

Her first thought when she saw the man settled with casual arrogance on the corner of Helen's desk was that he was just another hood on the take for some free legal advice. Her second thought, however—and this one distressed her—was that he was the most blatantly sexy man she'd ever seen. He was rough-cut, ragged, and, she'd bet her last paycheck, randy.

As she watched, he flashed a smile. Though that smile was directed at Helen, January felt the effects of his sure, cocky grin like a hard throbbing. And that throbbing was in places Helen liked to talk and giggle about and January avoided mentioning at all costs.

Much as she wanted to ignore him and let Helen send him on his way, January couldn't stop herself from staring.

There was so much to see.

He was a big man, tall and lean, but firmly muscled. He wore a black sleeveless T-shirt that both revealed and concealed provocative expanses of tanned, sleek skin and broad, toned chest. His jeans, tight and low on his hips, were faded almost white, and a wish and a prayer seemed to be the two strongest threads holding them together. His hair, as thick as the charm he was pouring on Helen and as black as his scuffed biker boots, was long enough to make his mother—if he had a mother—blush a deep red as she wondered where she'd gone wrong with her son. A diamond earring winked wickedly at January when, with a large, long-fingered hand, he brushed the wind-whipped strands behind his left ear and away from his face.

What a face.

His overall appearance suggested he kept rough company, yet his nose was so Nordic and straight, it made her wonder how he'd escaped having it broken. His cheekbones were high and strong, his jaw a study in stubbornness and totally at odds with the fluid mobility of his full lips. Lips that promised pleasure . . . and compliance . . . and trouble.

January watched with a catch in her breath as he twisted at the hip, planted his hands on the top of Helen's desk, and leaned toward her, grinning another one of those intimate, suggestive grins. Helen beamed like a schoolgirl on her first trip behind the bleachers. She seemed to consider denying whatever request he was making, then succumbed to another killer smile. Touching a hand to her neon-bright hair, she picked up the phone.

Even though she knew what would happen next, January jumped when Helen's voice purred over the speaker. "Ms. Stewart, there's a gentl—"

"The answer is no, Helen," January broke in quickly, before Helen could finish asking for what she strongly sensed would be a colossal mistake from the start. "You know my bank account can't handle another freebie, no matter how tight he wears his pants."

"Oh, he'll be so pleased you were able to make room on your schedule," Helen cooed, studiously avoiding looking January's way. She smiled sweetly at Mr. Tight Pants, who turned his head and met January's gaze through the glass wall.

Nothing had prepared January for those eyes. They were a shocking, liquid blue. Heartbreak blue. She should have thought of ice; instead, she felt a flame. A low, slow licking flame as he held her motionless with his gaze alone, filling her senses with an intense, intimate heat. A heat so mesmerizing it nearly suppressed another more powerful emotion. Panic. She felt it like a frigid blast of winter wind that gained velocity as it swept nearer.

She knew him. She was certain she knew him! But from where? And more importantly, from when? Then it hit her.

Michael Hayward.

Oh, God. As her heart beat heavily, she fought the fear that threatened to take over.

Michael Hayward. His name was synonymous with pain.

She felt her palms grow damp and the suffocating ache in her chest grow tighter. How, she wondered, after all these years, had he found her? And what did he want with her? He was an important and powerful journalist now. People listened when he spoke, believed what he wrote.

She made herself hold his gaze, searching for some sign of recognition on his part. She found none. Her pulse leaped with hope. Could that be? She'd swear by the look in his eyes that his interest was present, not past.

Her mind raced for more reasons to support her conclusion. He couldn't have found her by her name. She'd changed it. *She'd* changed. It had been fifteen years. She'd been thirteen then, a gangly stick of an awkward kid, whom she prayed she no longer had any resemblance to, either physically or emotionally. He'd been a cocky twenty-three-year-old reporter, out to take on the world at anyone's expense. At her expense. Hers and her mother's.

No, she decided finally but without much relief. He didn't recognize her. So why was he there?

It wasn't worth taking the chance to find out.

Forcefully tearing her gaze free of his, she swiveled in her chair so her back was to the wall of glass. She whipped off her glasses and sat forward. Fighting a sickening wave of nausea, she spoke in to the phone again, trying to keep her voice from shaking.

"Helen, I want you to listen to me," she said with as much calm authority as she could force past her tightly constricted vocal cords. "I don't care how you do it, but get rid of him."

"Of course, Ms. Stewart," Helen replied cheerfully. "I'll send him right in."

January's heart dropped like a stone.

She drew in a deep breath and listened as her office door opened, then closed.

Slowly, she turned to face him, promising herself as she did so that if she was still practicing law when Mr. Hayward got through with her, she was going to do it. She was going to fire Helen. Really.

Lulled by the sultry, almost tropical heat Helen Morgan had spoon-fed him in the waiting room, Michael Hayward had to suppress a shiver when he strode into January Stewart's office.

He'd long ago learned that in his business, his looks were as much of an asset as his ability to cut to the heart of a matter. Neither vain nor blind to the reactions he normally received from women, he routinely used those reactions to open doors. And he used them with the same ease with which he wore his dark good looks and too-long hair.

But January Stewart's reaction, he soon found out, was nowhere near the norm.

He offered her a tentative smile.

She met it with a distinct glacial glare.

Ice, he thought with mild amusement, should be so cold.

So he had tried for a smile and failed. Not a good start, but not the end of the movie either. Yet when he extended his hand and she ignored it, too, he could almost see the closing credits rolling.

If resistance were a color, he mused, appraising her with interest, it would be the color of her eyes. The beautiful dark eyes that had shot fire during the impassioned speech he'd heard her deliver a week before were as cold and unyielding as diamonds today.

"I know this is an imposition, Ms. Stewart," he

began, undaunted, "and I appreciate the fact that you agreed to see me on such short notice."

"I've only a few minutes, Mr. Hayward."

The lady was resistant all right, he thought. Resistant and hostile. Intrigued, he tipped one corner of his mouth up in a half-grin. "So you know who I am."

"One would have to live in a vacuum not to know who you are and what you do," she said bluntly.

His grin widened. "I'm past the point of losing sleep over low opinions of my work, but at least it explains your cool reception. Not one of my biggest fans, I take it."

Caution or relief, he wasn't sure which, colored her expression. More intrigued than ever, Michael watched as, with obviously staged patience, she folded her delicate hands together on the top of her desk.

"I *have* read your work, Mr. Hayward," she said, gazing at him with bland tolerance, "but I have neither the time nor the inclination to discuss it."

"That's a *nolo contendere* plea if I ever heard one, Counselor," he said, playing for another smile. He wasn't surprised when she didn't deliver. Disappointed, maybe, but not surprised.

She glanced at her austere, black-banded watch, then back at him. "I'm expecting a client in fifteen minutes, and I still have to prepare for the appointment. If there's something you want to discuss with me, I suggest you get to it."

He couldn't help it. He grinned again. At her businesslike brusqueness, at the nearly Victorian starchiness of her pristine white blouse and sedate navy business suit. Already this lady was an enigma to him. He found himself itching to crack that cold, crisp demeanor she had wrapped around herself like prison bars. He was way past merely wanting to know if the passion she'd nearly exploded with during her speech last week was all consumed by cause and purpose. Now he needed to know, needed to know if any of that passion was left over for more pleasurable pursuits. Man–woman pursuits.

When he wanted so much more, he'd be damned if he'd settle for an icy reception. In spite of the fact that she hadn't offered an invitation, he eased himself comfortably into the chair opposite her antique oak desk.

"You were really something at the conference last week," he said sincerely. "Fire and ice . . . that's what I thought of when I watched you. Fired up with determination, iced over with a single-minded purpose."

"You were at the conference on child abuse? That's how you know me?"

He shrugged. "You never know where you'll find a story." He paused, watching with interest as something that looked suspiciously like relief flashed across her dark eyes, then continued. "It's true that the topic isn't a pretty one, but I got the picture that the National Committee for the Prevention of Child Abuse doesn't care about pretty. They care about impact and results. Your keynote address got just that. I don't think you left a dry eye in the house."

She studied him for a long moment before replying. "I was asked to deliver a message that needed to be heard."

He smiled. "Well, take it from me, January. You delivered. Man, did you deliver."

He leaned back in the chair, remembering how she'd looked that day. She'd been a tall, slim bundle of ready-to-detonate dynamite. Her eyes had flashed with emotion, and her shoulder-length walnut brown hair had swung in counterpoint to her animated gestures. She'd spoken with heartfelt outrage, stirring and moving even the most jaded among the audience. He hadn't been prepared for the impact she'd had on him . . . professionally or physically.

Watching her now, he decided she was somewhat more relaxed than when he'd first walked into her office. Still, she shot another impatient glance at her watch.

"I'm glad you found my speech enlightening," she said, "but I fail to see why it brought you here. If I remember correctly, what you write is more in the line of exposés or upbeat human interest articles. My cause is hardly your style, Mr. Hayward."

She was dismissing him, he realized, pure and simple.

"Look, I'm sorry," he said, trying again to draw a bead on what it was about him that turned her off. "I don't usually make business appointments on the spur of the moment or looking like this, but I wasn't working today, and I just happened to cruise down this street—"

"Cruise?"

He nodded toward the window behind her, where a monster bike took up the bulk of a parking space next to the curb. "She's mine. Speaking of style, I never thought that a bike was my style either until I did a piece on a biker gang last year. But that's one of the great things about life, isn't it? It's full of surprises. Before I knew it, I was hooked on the wind-in-my-hair, bugs-in-my-teeth fantasy, you know?" She stared stonily at him. Again, his attempt at humor fell flat. "No. I guess you don't know. Anyway, I was riding by and recognized the address as yours—"

"Why would you know my address?"

There it was again, he thought, that unease he'd initially sensed, only now he could put a name to what he was seeing in her eyes. Panic. Definitely panic. He wanted to decipher the cause, but a puzzling need to reassure her outdistanced his curiosity.

"You're in the phone book," he said. "I've been meaning to call and set up an appointment, but, like I said, when I realized where I was today . . ." He paused as he saw his clumsy attempt to put her at ease was futile. "This is not going well at all, is it? Could we start over?" When her eyes indicated an unqualified "no," he frowned, then snapped his fingers. "It's the way I look, right?"

Something had warned him she would not be impressed by biker boots and jeans, no matter how "Richard Geerish" his brother, Rob, told him he looked in them. He'd decided to chance meeting her anyway, because another little something had told him January Stewart wasn't the kind of woman who would be particularly impressed by a well-knotted tie and imported leather loafers either.

Nothing had told him she wouldn't be impressed at all.

At thirty-eight, he was a little old to suffer through a case of bruised adolescent pride, but the longer he thought about it, the more he realized that was what this was stacking up to be.

Even as he studied her, wondering what his next approach should be, cool detachment crowded out all other emotions on her face as she met his assessing gaze.

"I'm very busy, Mr. Hayward. Please state your business."

He ran a hand through his hair in frustration. This was beginning to feel like a dead end. He couldn't remember the last time he'd had to beg to be allowed to feature someone in an article. He sure as hell didn't need the aggravation. But he kept thinking back to the way she'd been last week, and he kept wanting to feel the heat from this lady's fire.

"Okay," he said, deciding to play it her way. "You want short and simple, you got it. I liked what you said and the way you said it. So I took it upon myself to look you up. And to look up your bio."

Though she blinked slowly and did not alter her expression, he sensed her panic kick into overdrive. Baffled, he nonetheless pressed on, making a mental note to reread his file on her more carefully. Maybe he'd missed something, something the lady didn't want him to know. Something not so sweet in her pure-as-honey profile, which should have ended with a nomination for sainthood.

He'd never been afraid to bait when he smelled a story. He didn't hesitate now. "Frankly, you sounded too good to be true. So good, in fact, that the thought crossed my mind that your list of credits may have been hand-fed to the media to foster a certain image."

He watched with interest as her slender fingers tightened to a white-knuckled grip around each other.

"You have all the earmarks of an up-and-coming attorney," he continued relentlessly. "Of someone maybe trying to make a name for herself as a champion of the children. Bleeding-heart liberals are in vogue this year, I understand. The new legislature moving into office at the beginning of the year could be highly impressed by you. An appointment to the attorney general's office would be no small coup, would it, January?"

"Your conclusions are interesting, Mr. Hayward," she said in an evenly modulated tone that did not equate with the anger he knew she must be feeling. "But they are without validity or value. If you'll excuse me—"

"January," he interrupted, admiring the poise with which she controlled herself. He hadn't meant a word of that drivel, but she'd provoked him, dammit. Feeling like a major-league rat for harassing her, he backed off. "I was wrong. Wrong in spades. You are the most real lady I believe I've ever encountered. An honest to goodness, twentieth-century heroine."

Her brown eyes relayed impatience and suspicion. "Your point, Mr. Hayward?"

Damn, but she was one uptight lady. So uptight, she didn't recognize he was sincere.

"It's Michael, January, and my point is that it was your unquestionable sincerity that piqued my interest." He tactfully refrained from mentioning that it was also a great pair of legs that had piqued his curiosity about her as a woman. In fact, he'd become more than a little preoccupied with thoughts about those legs. "I'd like to write a series of articles about you and your cause."

After what seemed like an eternity but in reality was only a moment, she filled the expectant silence with one small, nonnegotiable word. "No." Then she showed him to the door.

Two

Statue-still, January stared out the window and watched Michael Hayward ride away in the roar of his cycle and a cloud of city dust.

Once he was out of sight, it was business as usual again on the streets. A gust of Indian summer wind stirred debris along the litter-strewn pavement. Nearby, a few street dwellers congregated near a cracked concrete tub full of barely blooming chrysanthemums, which Helen single-handedly kept alive with military determination and daily waterings.

Outwardly, January maintained her own status quo. On the inside, though, she felt as though she were splintering into a million jagged pieces.

She'd be kidding herself if she believed she'd seen the last of Michael Hayward. He'd be back. She knew he'd be back. What was she going to do then?

"All right." Helen charged into the small office without preamble or permission. "Spill it and I don't mean tomorrow."

On another day January might have found humor in Helen's drill sergeant delivery. Another time she might have been able to give back as much sass as she got and tell Helen to mind her own business. But this wasn't just another day. This was the day her past had caught up with her. And this was the day she had a problem she simply couldn't handle alone.

"Come in and shut the door," she said quietly.

She hesitated, then turned in her chair and met the older woman's eyes.

"Oh, dear," Helen murmured, her scowl transforming instantly to concern. "Looks like you'd better talk to me, honey."

Dodging Helen's probing gaze, January studied her hands, which she'd again clasped tightly together on top of her desk. It took all of her will to keep them from shaking. "I don't know where to start," she said frankly.

That uncharacteristic lapse of confidence was not lost on Helen. "Try, 'Once upon a time,'" she suggested kindly. "It's usually quite effective."

January watched Helen settle into the chair Michael Hayward had just vacated. She drew in a ragged breath. "I talked with my mother last night."

"That's nice," Helen said, clearly baffled by the choice of topics. Then a thought struck her. "Oh, honey, is there something wrong with Monica?"

Though her relationship with her mother was distant, January felt a protective sort of love for her, and Helen knew it. "No," January said softly. "No, she's fine."

"Then why are we talking about Monica, sweetie?" Helen's tone was admonishing but gentle. "I could have sworn your present state of mind had something to do with the black-leather–trimmed dream machine that just strolled out of here."

Dream? January pinched her eyes shut and fought a shudder. Michael Hayward wasn't a dream.

He was her worst nightmare come back to haunt her.

Struggling for composure, she resumed the study of her hands. They no longer felt like they were attached to her body. Nothing felt attached. She clasped them tighter, afraid that if she let go, she would fly apart and ricochet in a thousand different directions. Wouldn't he love that? Wouldn't he love knowing he had this effect on her?

"You've never asked me about my father," she managed to say finally, determined to see this through. "Haven't you wondered about him? Why I've never mentioned him?"

Helen's mouth twisted in frustration, but her concern obviously took over. "I've never asked you about your father because I've always sensed it was something you didn't want to talk about. But yes, I've wondered about him."

"He was a drinker," January said bluntly. "A mean one."

Restless, uncomfortable with the memories, she pushed out of her chair. Hugging her arms tightly to her body, she faced the window. "To make a long story short, my mother and I were his favorite targets. Until the summer I turned thirteen. By then Mother didn't have any fight left in her, and it became more fun for him to vent all of his anger on me."

The silence that settled over the small office could have filled a courtroom. It seemed to stretch to the length of a life sentence before January forced herself to meet Helen's gaze and hold it. "One night I decided I wasn't going to let him . . . hurt me anymore. I fought back . . . and I killed him."

The empathy she saw in Helen's eyes filled her with an unqualified rush of love and gave her the courage to go on with her story.

"Needless to say, the incident caused quite a stir. It made great headlines and even greater copy. A tragic small-town murder. A study in poverty and pain. The press lapped it up. There was, of course, the sympathy issue, the thirteen-year-old child forced beyond her limits of endurance, the mother caught between grief over the loss of her husband and fear for her daughter's future. Not to mention the intrigue attached to the fact that he'd been shot with his own handgun."

"Oh, honey." Helen's voice was clogged with the emotion January struggled to keep from her own. The older woman's eyes swam with tears as she gazed at January with so much compassion, it felt like a physical embrace.

Helen had always been a toucher. It was as natural as breathing for her to open her arms and draw someone close when they were hurting. Past experience, however, had taught her that January would reject the gesture. Yet today, in the wake of Michael Hayward's earthquaking reentry into her life, January found herself wishing Helen would let go of the restraint she so notoriously lacked and hold her. Just hold her.

To combat the wanting, she turned back to the window.

"I suspected soon after I started working for you," Helen said, "that you'd had it rough as a kid."

Her comment spun January around with a start.

The older woman smiled. "No, honey, you don't wear it like a badge, but it doesn't take a rocket scientist to figure out why you shy away from men, from physical displays of affection. Or even why you're so dedicated to your work with children." She paused, then pressed on carefully. "Jan, you want to tell me what brought this all out today?"

Encouraged by Helen's kindness, January continued. "As I said, after his . . . after my father's death, the press had a field day." She tried but couldn't conceal her emotions any longer. "One reporter in particular played it for every word he could badger into print. He humiliated and sensationalized and hounded us, as if we were nothing more than players in some cheap drama. To him we existed solely for the purpose of his exploitation."

"Oh, good Lord," Helen muttered as comprehension dawned. She touched a trembling hand to her mouth. "It was him, the reporter. It was Hayward, wasn't it?"

The knot in January's breast clenched, coiling tight at the mention of his name. "He was a nobody then. No one had ever heard of Michael Hayward. But he had the fire. And the drive. We were his first big assignment. Imagine, having your life reduced to being someone's 'assignment.'" She shook herself mentally but couldn't keep the panic from encroaching on the anger.

"Honey," Helen began uneasily, "what does he want?"

"What he always wants," she said coldly. "A story."

"A story? A follow-up after all these years?"

She laughed, too loud, too fast, but her control had finally slipped, and she just couldn't stop it. "That's the irony. There's always irony, didn't you know? Always some twist to knock you off kilter, always some little spin to keep you off balance." Meeting Helen's concerned gaze, she regained her composure and explained. "He doesn't realize who I am. He doesn't know who he's stumbled onto. He thinks I'm just some Pollyanna attorney out to set the world right. He heard me speak last week at the conference and was—in his words—taken by my sincerity and sense of purpose."

"Most people are," Helen said softly, calmingly.

January looked back toward the window. "Most people don't have the ability to destroy me. Michael Hayward does."

"But if he doesn't recognize you, I don't see the problem—"

"Helen, he's a journalist! A relentless, ruthless one. He didn't know me today, but it won't be long before he figures it out. He's already digging. He told me so. A name change and a fifteen-year time lapse aren't a lot of cover between the present and a past that could destroy everything I've worked for."

"Honey, what happened with your father was terrible and tragic, but you were a child, a victim. No one would hold you responsible for that."

She shook her head emphatically, then pinched her eyes closed. Concentrating on deep, even breaths, she called on her physical control to calm her emotionally. "It messed me up for a while, Helen. It messed everything up. Mom was in bad shape for a long time. She couldn't give me what I needed then. I—I didn't know what I needed. I just knew what I wanted. Attention. And I knew how to get it." Hugging herself again in an unconscious gesture of self-protection, she paced behind her desk. "I got mixed up with a bad crowd. I . . . I did things, many things I regret now but couldn't stop myself from doing then."

"You were a child."

She met the kindness in Helen's eyes with cynicism. "I have a record, Helen. I don't have to tell you what would happen if that fact were uncovered. Politicians, though not always lily-white, want their public servants to be. They wouldn't like it if they found out about me. Everything that's important, my work for the children, the advocate service, would simply be no more if my federal block grant money was pulled. And they'd pull it in a minute rather than face a scandal."

"Why are you so sure Michael Hayward would expose you if he did find out who you are?"

January's voice, like her eyes, grew hard. "Because I lived what he did to us. I know how he operates. If he uncovers my identity, he'll stop at nothing to bring the entire ugly story to life again. Even if he stopped with the story of the murder, too much publicity could jeopardize the federal funding. Without it, I couldn't do the legal aide work. I can't risk it. And neither can my mother. Exposure would kill her. It took her a long time to get her life back together. She and Howard are happy now. He's a state representative. Can you imagine what association with me, the old me, would do to his career?"

Helen considered her carefully. "Admittedly, you have a potential problem here, sweetie, but remember, you are not the same confused, troubled little girl you were fifteen years ago. Michael Hayward has those same fifteen years on him too. He could have changed. He may not be the user you remember. He didn't impress me as being vindictive or cruel, and that's what he'd have to be if he uncovered your story and brought it to light."

"Don't kid yourself, Helen. Behind that pretty face is a self-serving jackal. Now you listen to me. If he calls or comes by again, I don't want to see or talk to him."

Helen sighed deeply. "I don't think he's going to go away that easily."

As much for herself as for Helen, January remained adamant. "He'll go. If he's told no often enough, he'll move on to greener pastures."

"Call me crazy, but something he said when he left tells me that a little word like *no* isn't going to put a dent in that man's determination to see you again."

January braced herself. "What did he say?"

Helen smiled tentatively. "You sure you want to know?"

"Helen!"

"All right. He walked out of your office, leaned back against the door, shook his head, and said—sounding a little awed, I might add—'She's one tough lady.' Then he laughed and winked, and in the deepest, most confident voice I've ever heard, added, 'But I'm tougher.' Then he said, 'I'll see you again real soon,' and he left."

January's heart lurched but she held her ground. "If he calls, I'm out. If he comes by, I'm busy. It's just that simple. He'll get tired of the runaround and go away."

"I don't know," Helen said, shaking her head. "And I wonder if you might be making a mistake, Jan. If he's as tenacious as his reputation indicates, he won't quit until he gets his story. You might be better off cooperating with him. If you give him what he wants, he won't be forced to do his own research. You could be slitting your throat by being so resistant."

Although she had considered that possibility, she'd dismissed it as unsound logic. "I don't think so. The more he knows, the more he'll want to know. I can't risk the contact with him."

"And what if his interest is more personal than professional?"

Something in Helen's tone set January's senses humming. With a look, she brushed the notion off as ridiculous.

"You don't think you'd be his type?" Helen asked. "Don't make book on it, sweetie. There was a certain awareness in his voice when he left here, a certain interest. You're a challenge. And a challenge is something a man like that finds hard to resist." She paused for effect, then added, "He's very attractive."

She looked at Helen sharply. "He almost destroyed my life once. He could easily do it again. Please keep that in mind if he sashays back here oozing charm and flashing that bad-boy grin."

"Oh, I'll keep it in mind, all right. I just hope you know what you're doing."

January watched Helen leave, trying to convince herself that she knew exactly what she was doing, that she was in control of this situation. Years ago she'd made a conscious decision to take charge of her own life, and she'd done it. That decision had eventually propelled her past the ordeal of her father's abuse and his death, and had steered her toward a career in law. Her control had always seen her through her most difficult cases.

In more ways than one, Michael Hayward represented a threat to that control. He could destroy her career. She shuddered. He could destroy her.

A week later, January glanced quickly around the emptying courtroom as she gathered her documents and shoved them into her briefcase. She was pleased with the judge's ruling but not with her performance. It had been sadly lacking, for she needed too much of her concentration to block thoughts of Michael Hayward.

She hadn't been as successful the previous night . . . or any of the past seven nights, for that matter. More than once she'd lain awake well past midnight damning him for showing up after all these years. Damning him for being so dangerous . . . so dangerously attractive. And damning herself for finding him so.

She wanted to deny it. She'd tried. Half of last

night, she'd tried. But somewhere around one A.M. she'd given up and admitted the truth. Despite the threat he represented, she *was* attracted to him. That knowledge frightened her as much as the thought of what he could do to her professionally.

For the first time since she'd decided on a career in law, he made her think of herself as a woman, naked and stripped of the barrier she had long ago erected against men. And he made her aware of him as she had never let herself be aware of a man. He was so—so male. Her stomach clenched at the memory of the erotic dream that had awakened her after she'd finally fallen asleep. She *never* had erotic dreams! At least she hadn't until now.

She snapped her briefcase and her memory closed, then raked a shaking hand through her hair. It wasn't fair. She'd learned long ago that life wasn't fair. She accepted that, but she'd paid her dues. How much more did she have to contribute? And why did Michael Hayward have to appear at a time in her life when she was having difficulty dealing with the future she'd carved out in stone? A future that called for her to go it alone, and now looked as bleak and barren as the bed she crawled into by herself every night.

Frustrated, she hefted her briefcase with one hand and tucked the overflow of paperwork under her arm. Shouldering her purse, she headed for the back of the now empty courtroom. She'd cleared the doors and was walking briskly down the hall toward the bank of elevators before she realized she had a shadow.

She didn't have to turn around to know who was behind her. Even in this sea of people, she recognized Michael Hayward's scent from that afternoon in her office. It was subtle, a little musky, a lot male, and she had awakened that morning wrestling with the admission that it had lingered in her memory far too long.

She recognized, too, the same sinking sensation she'd felt when he'd sauntered into her office and taken command of the air space surrounding them both.

"This has got to stop, Mr. Hayward," she said without slowing her stride or turning around.

"But it hasn't even started," he replied with just enough sugar to sweeten, just enough threat to take note, and, she noticed, without an ounce of denial.

How could he deny it? He left messages daily on her answering machine. Her *home* answering machine. Fresh roses waited on her desk when she arrived for work each morning, as well as a fistful of pink slips Helen delighted in waving under her nose every time she walked in the door.

With grim reluctance she stopped and faced him. Immediately, she regretted it. The only trace of the outlaw who'd bulldozed Helen was the classically handsome face, the clear blue eyes, and the devastatingly confident grin.

Gone were the biker boots and low-riding jeans. In their place were custom-made loafers and charcoal flannel trousers. Although the physique-revealing black T-shirt had been replaced by a crisp white shirt and a navy jacket, there was no hiding the measure of the man beneath them. His hair was neatly combed, and its length enhanced rather than detracted from his good looks. Even the earring was less offensive than it was intriguing.

She loathed herself for noticing that, and the way the bright fluorescent lights cast blue-black highlights in his hair. And she hated that standing next to her, he looked down on her from a good three-inch height advantage, which most men didn't have when she wore heels that elevated her five feet eight inches even more.

"If you look at me like that much longer, January," he drawled, flashing that bad-boy grin of his, "I'm going to have to consider it an invitation."

Embarrassed, she tore her gaze from his and resumed her escape toward the elevators. "If you keep hounding me like this, Hayward," she threatened over her shoulder, "I'm going to have to consider it harassment."

Less than a step behind her he answered amiably, "There is a solution, you know."

"Yeah. It's called an injunction."

He laughed. The sound was deep and rich and, unaccountably, it wrapped around her senses like a soft warm glove.

"There's always that," he agreed, "but what I had in mind was dinner."

The elevator opened just as she reached it. She couldn't step inside fast enough. He followed her, along with a crush of people heading for the first floor. When the doors had closed and the dust had settled, January found herself wedged in a back corner. Michael was facing her, his forearm propped on the wall above her head, his body forming an effective barrier from the jostling crowd. A barrier or a trap. She wasn't yet sure which. One thing she was sure of was that this was going to be the longest elevator ride of her life.

Oddly, though, she didn't feel threatened by him. She felt uneasy, yes. Tense, definitely. And she was far too aware of the pleasant way his breath feathered across the top of her head, of the radiant, musky heat his body generated, and of his eyes watching her with gentle amusement.

"Come on, Counselor, lighten up," he said with the ease of an accomplished flirt. "You have to eat, so what do you say?"

Shifting her slipping bundle of legal briefs, she

gave him a clipped, decisive "no," then added a begrudging, "thank you."

Undaunted, he masterfully relieved her of her heavy briefcase. Before she could utter a protest, he distracted her with his next comment.

"You know, you were really something in there. But then, that didn't surprise me given your win–loss record in court."

She wasn't sure which threw her the most—the fact that he had been in the courtroom, or the fact that he had researched her court record.

"I got the feeling this case was really special for you," he added.

Unwittingly, she reacted to his observation. "They're all special." Jeremy Garner and his uncle had become special the moment Ronald Garner had retained January to fight for permanent custody of Jeremy.

"But you were bucking the system on this one, weren't you?" he asked.

She frowned up at him, trying to decide if he was simply insightful, well informed, or playing the probing reporter.

"Jeremy was temporarily placed with his uncle a little over a year ago by the Department of Human Services. By law, the state's ultimate goal in a situation like this is to return Jeremy to his natural parents after they've participated in a treatment program."

"But you agree with the uncle that the state's solution isn't in Jeremy's best interest."

"If you were there, then you heard. But to answer your question, if I didn't agree, I wouldn't have taken the case. I don't like 'bucking the system,' as you put it, but this time the system was wrong. Human Services had Jeremy's interest at heart too. It's just that sometimes, given staff shortages and unmanageable case loads, perspective can get lost in the paper shuffle. The Garners are habitual offenders. Jeremy is five years old and has been in foster homes for almost three out of those five years. Ron is Jeremy's last hope."

Michael appeared to think about that for a moment before challenging her. "But according to the State's case, the Garners are rehabilitated. You don't think they could have changed their ways?"

She didn't want to argue the case again, but for some reason heard herself answering just the same. "For their sake, I hope they have. But I'm not concerned with the Garners. I'm concerned with Jeremy, and he deserves a chance to have something he's never had—stability, love, and the security to get him past his parents' neglect and abuse."

Michael's silence seemed both thoughtful and condemning. She didn't want to care what he thought of her, but she did.

"Look, Hayward, the case has been tried. I don't have to defend my motives again to you. The Garners had several chances. Now Jeremy is entitled to a chance of his own. He'll get it with Ron."

"Whoa, Counselor. I'm not judging you. I'm just trying to get a bead on what makes you tick. And believe it or not, there was a compliment in all that somewhere. I'm intrigued by the way you work, by your perspective. It's almost as if you know where these people have been, and what brought them to this point."

She quickly looked away. He'd managed to strike a nerve and at the same time get too close to the truth she was hiding. It wouldn't do to give him the advantage of knowing it.

"Hey," he said, his gentle, sincere tone urging her gaze back to his, "it was difficult for you, wasn't it? Court, I mean."

"It's always difficult."

"Which brings me to the reason I'm here. The

way I've got it figured, you're a very busy woman. You haven't had an extra minute to answer my messages. So I thought I'd save you the trouble of calling me back by meeting you face-to-face."

She sighed heavily and prayed the elevator would reach the ground floor sometime in this century. "You're right, I am busy. But I didn't answer your messages because I did not *want* to answer your messages. I'm not interested in doing the article. I thought I'd made myself clear."

"Crystal clear." His eyes gleamed with an intriguing mixture of curiosity and candor. "What I don't understand is why. Is it just the article you're resistant to?" His voice, like his laughter, was soft and compelling. "Or is it me?"

Even more compelling was the thread of vulnerability she heard in his softly posed question. She met his eyes and felt her restraint melting, until a stunning rush of reality hit her broadside. She'd forgotten for a moment who she was dealing with. Not only was he an accomplished flirt, he was an indiscriminate user who knew how to play his game well. She couldn't trust him. Her eyes must have telegraphed her thoughts, because his expression hardened.

"I frighten you," he said with both wonder and denial. "Why?"

"Don't be absurd," she said, wishing he weren't correct.

The doors finally opened onto the lobby, freeing her from the scrutiny of his narrowed eyes. She shouldered around him and through the crowd filing out of the elevator.

He caught up with her in one long stride. "Why do I intimidate you, January?"

"You do *not* intimidate me. And I'm not resistant to the article. I'm just busy. I don't have room on my calendar."

"Room for me or room for the article?"

She pushed through the door that opened onto Pearl Street.

He squeezed through with her and deferred to his original argument. "Don't tell me you didn't schedule in dinner."

The autumn air had a crisp bite to it as it hit her full in the face. Her reply had a bit of a bite too. "I'll grab a sandwich at home."

"Then I'll drive you."

She rounded on him. "Will you just stop!" she shouted, then realized what he'd accomplished. He'd gotten to her. She couldn't let that happen. Worse, she couldn't afford to let him know he had the capability.

A gust of wind skittered up the courthouse steps, tumbling a swirl of fallen leaves in its wake as she appealed to him once more. "Look, you are wasting your time and mine. Just let it alone, okay?"

The same wind that chased the leaves and played havoc with her skirt, gently ruffled his dark hair away from his face. Startled again by his sheer physical perfection, she forced her gaze over his shoulder, aware as she did so that he was studying her with a deep frown.

"I guess you've had a long day," he said in a tone suggesting both concern and acquiescence. "You don't need me to make it any longer."

He lifted a hand to her face and without hesitation or request carefully tugged a windblown strand of hair from the corner of her mouth.

She flinched reflexively, though there was nothing frightening about his touch. Nothing repelling, no aggression. It was surprisingly gentle. Surprisingly nice.

"January?" His eyes, when she met them, were full of questions. "Are you all right?"

Unnerved by the effect he had on her, she could only nod.

"Come on then. I'll walk you to your car."

"Really, that won't be necessary," she said, and reached for her briefcase. His cool gaze met and held hers as their fingers touched, then tangled on the leather handle.

The contact was far too potent. She felt a tingle that should have been fear, but wasn't. She felt a wonder that shouldn't have been, but was. In that moment, she knew only one thing with undeniable certainty. She had to get away from him.

Fighting the urge to snatch the briefcase out of his grip, she held on stubbornly.

With considerable reluctance he finally let go.

"Good-bye, Mr. Hayward."

Before he could voice another protest, she hurried down the steps to the curb. At that moment she would have sold her soul to the devil if he would only have gotten her a cab.

The devil wasn't about to deliver. Not today. Not at this hour.

The traffic was thick and steady. Checking her watch, she groaned, then swore softly. She'd probably end up standing there for an hour before she ever saw a cab, let alone got one to stop.

The sound of slow, confident footsteps behind her ended any feeble notion that Michael had left her alone, or that the devil wasn't afoot after all.

"Forget where you parked your car?" he asked.

"I never said I had my car."

"You never said you didn't," he said, clearly as pleased as punch that he'd caught her in a lie of omission.

"I'll get a cab. I'll be fine."

"You'll be old," he countered with an easy smile, "before you get a cab in this town."

There was nothing she could say to that. She was already calculating the time it would take to get home. It added up to too much. But when she calculated the risk of being alone in a car with him, she decided she'd take her chances and wait for the cab. Maybe, if she ignored him, he'd go away.

Sure, she thought, and cowboys rode cows.

As he stood beside her, she was aware that he was quietly but obviously amused.

"You're really very good at this, you know," he remarked as they watched a steady stream of cars speed by.

She exhaled slowly, her patience near its threshold. "Good at what?"

"Executing a brush-off."

"If I'm so good, why isn't it working?"

"Damned if I know," he said, as if his own persistence amazed him. "I guess I just never learned to accept defeat gracefully. But then, I'm not altogether certain I've been defeated."

That was when the first raindrop fell. They looked toward the darkening sky at the same moment.

Her growl of exasperation earned her a lopsided grin.

"Right on cue," he said as if he'd masterminded the entire scenario.

"Nice trick," she said dryly. "What do you do for an encore? Walk on water?"

He laughed, and despite the autumn chill, January felt the same warm and intensely intimate sensation she'd experienced the first time she'd heard that sound.

"Too easy," he said. "I go for the really tough stuff . . . like rescuing stubborn women from themselves." He looked again toward the sky as a rapid succession of fat, splattering drops bombarded them. "Come on, Counselor." He grabbed her briefcase in one hand and her elbow in the other. "Like it or not, you've lost both the opening and the closing arguments on this case. My car's right over here. Let's make a run for it."

Three

Michael's younger brother, Rob, took affectionate sibling pleasure in pointing out that much of Michael's success was predicated on sheer dumb luck. As Michael guided a slightly wet, slightly prickly January Stewart into the passenger seat of his Bronco, he was—and quite happily—inclined to agree. Besides, at this point he'd accept any help he could get. If it took an autumn rainstorm to get the lady's undivided attention, hey, who was he to argue with mother nature?

He didn't want to argue with anyone. Especially not with January. He had other things in mind for her.

"You okay over there?" he asked, settling in behind the wheel.

She smoothed her wet skirt over her knees and looked straight ahead. "Fine."

"We'll have some heat here in a second," he promised, cranking on the ignition, then fiddling with the heater. "It'll take the chill off and dry us out a bit."

She fussed with her hair, not, he guessed, because she was concerned with her appearance, but because she needed something to do with her hands. He just knew she was afraid of him, and what frustrated him, what had him thoroughly irritated, was that he didn't have a clue as to why.

Dragging his fingers through his own wet hair, he tuned in the radio and watched her. She was as tense as a sinner in confession. For some reason, knowledge of that tension provoked him to increase it. He reached across her for her seat belt. She almost sprang through the roof when his arm "accidentally" brushed her breasts.

"Relax," he said, all innocence, as he fastened the belt at her hip. He paraphrased the signs posted on every major highway in the state. "It's the law. Can't have an officer of the court breaking the law, now can we?"

He was not surprised that she didn't smile. The quick, electric flash of panic in her eyes, however, momentarily stunned him. Then it was gone, and he was left wondering if he'd imagined it.

"So," he said, sliding back behind the wheel, "where's home?"

She blinked slowly. "Given the fact that you know my unlisted home phone number and my schedule well enough to show up at the courthouse, do you honestly expect me to believe you don't know where I live?"

He grinned. She had him there. Did he know where she lived? You damn betcha. And before he was through with her, he'd know a lot more. Like what it took to make her smile. And what the hell she was afraid of.

Turning on the windshield wipers, he set the Bronco in gear and pulled out of the lot. Hanging a left off Pearl, then eventually easing into the flow of traffic on the turnpike, he was content for the moment simply to have her in a position where she couldn't throw him out or run away.

The next fifteen minutes of silent driving gave him time to regroup and sift through his feelings. Since first seeing her at the conference, he hadn't been able to get her out of his head. When he'd gone to her office a week ago, he'd convinced himself he had a vested interest in writing an article and a passing interest in the lady herself. Passing, hell. It wasn't going away . . . at least not anytime soon. After meeting her face to face, he had finally given up trying to reason out why she intrigued him. She just did.

Rob would call it a mid-life crisis. Michael called it hell. Until now the ladies in his life had been as interested as he in no-strings, no-strain relationships. This one had him thinking of hearth and home and a hundred other sappy sentiments that led smart men into trouble.

Trouble was exactly what he was in.

He loved to listen to her talk. Even when she was telling him to get lost, her voice had a husky, silky resonance that made him think of black lace, dark midnights, and warm, giving flesh.

Oh yeah, she was one sexy lady too. He knew a lot of sexy ladies. This one, though, had a certain vulnerability, an innocence even, that was at intriguing odds with her legal prowess and the cool, confident persona she presented to the public. He wanted to crack that cold exterior. He wanted to make January thaw. Hell, he just wanted her, pure and simple. Only it wasn't so pure. And, he had to admit, it wasn't so simple. If it were just sexual, he could deal with it. But it wasn't. And that was the part that was giving him trouble.

"Why?"

He whipped his head around to look at her. She had been quiet for so long, her soft voice startled him. "I'm sorry. Did you say something?"

She met his eyes for a moment, then lifting her

chin, looked past the swishing windshield wipers to the wet highway and the curtain of dusk that cast the last of the afternoon in incandescent darkness. "Why are you doing this? Why don't you do us both a favor and just let it go?"

He let out a soft, self-derisive snort and swung onto the exit ramp. "I was just asking myself the same question." He didn't think she was ready for the truth. Not the whole of it anyway. So he offered a part of it that surprised even him.

"Something . . . something really profound struck a chord when I heard you speak. No wait, let me finish. I think maybe I saw something in you, heard something in what you said that I used to have inside myself. Conviction. Purpose. A whole fistful of determination to make a difference. You reminded me of myself ten years ago, and until I listened to your speech, I hadn't realized that somewhere along the way, I'd lost all those qualities that make you special."

He laughed. "Not exactly what you expected to hear, was it? Trust me, it wasn't exactly what I expected to say."

She was silent for a long time again. Finally, her brow furrowed as though she wasn't very pleased with her admission. She said, "I've found no lack of conviction in your work."

The compliment, he could tell, cost her. It made him smile, and it loosened his tongue even more. "I've been riding the wave of some earlier successes for too long now. I've been content, blindly so, to slide along with a much softer perspective. Fluff, even. I—I guess I finally realized that I don't like myself much these days. Not so much for the work I'm doing, but for what I'm not doing. When I went to that conference and heard you, really heard what you were saying, it hit me like a missile. It's time I get back on track. And I owe you for the eye-opener.

Once more, she was a long time responding. "I find it difficult to accept credit for a decision that was yours alone to make."

He grinned and thought of the date he'd broken for tonight, not to mention the assignment in Haiti he'd turned down because he hadn't wanted to leave without settling this business with her. "If you believe you weren't instrumental in some decisions I've made lately, you're dead wrong."

"I believe people have it within themselves to determine their own course of action."

"That may very well be, but in the right place, at the right time, a gentle nudge in the right direction has been known to move mountains. You moved my mountain, January," he teased in an intentional bid to lighten what was fast becoming a heavy conversation. "And now I'd like to move yours." He flashed her a grin full of innuendo.

She wanted to smile, he could see it in her eyes. But she fought off the urge as he suspected she was fighting off many other urges. "My mountain's just fine where it is, thank you."

"Is that another way of saying no, you still won't consider the article?"

She hesitated, then said softly, "That's another way of saying no."

He was prepared for that answer, but he had no intention of giving up. "Then I guess that gets us back to dinner. I know tonight's out, but would you consider letting me take you to the Flagstaff House on Saturday?"

She squeezed her eyes shut and let out a sigh of exasperation. "You just don't quit, do you?"

He pulled up in front of the modest house he'd driven by several times during the last week, and shut off the motor. Turning toward her, he propped one arm on the seat back and the other over the steering wheel. "No, January. I don't quit. Not when I'm going after something I really want."

An awareness flickered in her eyes that even the twilight of evening couldn't hide. "There . . ." She stopped and cleared her throat. "There must be a hundred more marketable topics you could write about."

He leaned toward her and deftly unfastened her seat belt. "I'm not talking about the article. I'm talking about you." Watching her profile, he let that settle before adding in a voice that sounded as thick as the suddenly pulsing flesh at his groin, "I've done everything but say it, so let's hear how it sounds. I want to see you, January. You fascinate me."

She sucked in a sharp breath. It made a thready little sound that added to the sweet discomfort in the lower part of his body.

"I frustrate you," she corrected him with conviction. "You're just not used to being told no."

He cupped her jaw in his hand and slowly turned her face toward him. "What I'm not used to is being turned inside out by the sound of one woman's voice, by the thought of how one woman's mouth would feel opened against mine." His gaze dropped to her mouth and lingered. When her small, pink tongue unconsciously slipped between her lips to wet them, he damn near exploded. "Do you think about that too, January? Do you think about what it would be like with me?"

She seemed to wilt, to go all soft and yearning right before his eyes. Then she swallowed hard and met his gaze with a fire in her eyes that even the night's rain wouldn't have doused. "You're out of line, Hayward."

He sighed deeply. "I know. I just don't know what to do about it. I'm coming on like a stag during the rutting season, aren't I? I'm sorry. I really wanted to take this slow. But being around you is like some grueling exercise in self-restraint."

"Restraint," she whispered in a thin voice, "is not a word I would have used in relationship to you."

Hearing a certain gentling, sensing a tentative yielding, he slid his hand into the wealth of heavy sable hair at the nape of her neck. "I want to kiss you, January. Would you let me?"

She shook her head, but without much conviction.

He touched a finger to her cheek, forcing her to look at him. "Don't send a kitten to do a cat's work, Counselor," he warned softly. "If you really mean no, you'll have to be more convincing than that."

When she swallowed hard yet said nothing, he pressed the issue gently. "Just once. Only once . . ."

Her eyes were big and round and uncertain as he lowered his mouth to hers. "No, baby," he whispered, dropping a tender kiss of introduction at the corner of her mouth. "Don't be afraid. I'd never hurt you."

But she was afraid. He could feel it beneath his hand as he stroked her hair, beneath his lips as they touched hers with such great care.

He wanted to ravage the hot, wet interior of her mouth; he wanted to tumble her to her back then and there. Her wants took priority, though. Her needs held greater value. He'd never been like this with a woman. And while his protective instincts baffled him, he didn't question that they were right on target. She needed to know that she could trust him.

So he delivered on his promise and took her mouth slowly, pressing against her soft, trembling lips without insistence.

She was sweet. Lord, so sweet. He could taste

her desire simmering beneath the surface, but kept his own hunger in check. He could also taste her fear. It was the latter he catered to. Catered to and wooed and finally won.

Much sooner than he wanted to, he pulled away. He smiled at her stunned expression. "And that, Ms. Stewart," he said, touching a finger to her parted lips, "is what you call exercising restraint."

She blinked slowly, a trait he was finding increasingly endearing. "And this," she said on a shaky breath, "just in case you miss the message, is what you call saying good-bye."

Grabbing blindly for her things, she shouldered her way out of the Bronco and ran through the rain to her door.

Michael sighed in resignation. It had been a long time since he'd chased a woman. In fact, the last woman he'd chased hadn't been a woman at all. She'd been ten years old and so had he, and they'd been playing tag in the school playground. But chase he did as he snagged her forgotten briefcase and headed up the walk to her front door.

He rang the bell several times before she answered it. By then, he was wet to his underwear. He figured it would give him an edge.

The door swung open. "What?" she snapped, ready to lay into him with both barrels.

He looked pathetic. He knew it. He played on it. Dangling her briefcase from one dripping finger, he brushed his soaking hair out of his eyes and gave her a lost-puppy grin. "Guess you'll have to let me in so I can dry out, huh? Sort of return the favor for the ride home?"

She glared at him. "Do *yourself* a favor, Hayward. Go away. Stay away."

He was still wearing that stupid grin when she unceremoniously relieved him of the briefcase and slammed the door in his face.

• • •

Michael counted to ten, walked stiffly to his Bronco, and drove directly to the nearest bar. Two beers and forty-five minutes worth of contemplation later, he was back. He didn't bother with the bell. He just hammered the hell out of her front door.

He was about ready to start yelling when from inside a hall light came on. He heard some fumbling, then the metallic glide of a safety latch being slipped into place, and finally, the click of a dead bolt. The door opened a crack. A pair of wary brown eyes stared at him from behind huge, round-rimmed glasses.

He didn't wait for her to speak. "I've got something to say to you, *Ms.* Stewart, and unless you want the whole damn neighborhood to hear it, I suggest you let me in."

Given the fact that he was madder than a dog who'd been stripped of his favorite bone, Michael was pleased with the outward calm with which he delivered his ultimatum. But when January hesitated and he sensed her next move, the rest came out on a growl. "So help me, Counselor, you slam this door in my face again, you'll regret it."

If his threat bothered her, she didn't show it. Her gaze met his in brief eye to eye combat before she expelled a patronizing sigh. Taking her sweet time about it, she unlatched and opened the door.

"Please make it quick," she said as she stood aside and shut the door behind him. "I've got a lot to do tonight."

Lord, but she was a piece of work, Michael thought. He ought to pound his soft head against a hard wall a couple of times for ever thinking she was vulnerable or sweet or sadly in need of a protector. The lady needed a protector like Ford needed another Edsel.

"You know what your problem is?" he asked, taking a superior swagger toward her. "You are an uptight, uptown, uppity little witch who can't stand the idea of a man—any man—exercising even the tiniest control over your actions!"

She faced him, arms crossed over her breasts in casual defiance, her expression a perfect study of bored tolerance. "You've been drinking."

"Two beers. I've had two lousy beers and as cold and frosty as they were, they didn't hold a candle to that facsimile of a kiss I had the bad judgment to think I wanted from you."

That, he knew, was hitting below the belt. But his pride was at stake here, and he wanted at the very least to insult hers.

He was cruising for a good shouting match, yet she wasn't about to deliver. He wanted to shake her until her teeth rattled. He wanted to kiss that benign scowl off her face. Then he wanted to make love to her until she was chanting his name like a prayer.

She should have had the good grace to look wounded, he thought. Or at least to call him a few names. But she just stood there, her chin held high, her hands cradling her elbows, waiting for the next insult to fly.

Irked with himself for even being there, irked with her for her lack of reaction—any reaction—he stepped toward her.

"Dammit, January," he muttered, raising a hand in frustration.

In a lightning move, she shrank away from him, covering her head protectively. "Don't . . . please don't."

Michael's hand froze in midair. Stunned by her violent reaction, he didn't understand its significance for a moment. She was waiting for a blow. She thought he was going to hit her.

His stomach lurched with revulsion as suddenly everything became clear. Too clear. Too sickeningly, disgustingly clear.

All along he'd sensed she was afraid of something. Now he knew what that something was . . . the back of his hand. Evidently some low-rent, slimy bastard had knocked her around, and she figured every man would give her the same treatment.

Fighting a rage unlike any he'd ever known, at the thought of someone, anyone, touching her violently, he lifted his hand onto its original destination and dragged it through his hair.

"January . . ." He swallowed hard and wondered where to go from here. "January, I don't hit women."

She drew a steadying breath, then looking embarrassed, pulled herself together. "I think you'd better leave."

Michael's gaze never left her face. It all made sense now, he mused, the iceberg shoulder, the crusty indifference. They were shields to hide the vulnerability, the shame, the fear that kept her from confiding in him. "Look at me, January."

He wasn't sure what emotion propelled her—defiance, pride, or sheer will—but she returned his gaze levelly.

"I am not like him. Whoever he was, I am not like him. Give me the chance to show you that. Give me the chance to show you how good it could be between us. That's all I want, the chance to show you something good."

She wasn't having any of it. Not tonight. Her eyes were suspiciously bright, and he could tell by the slight trembling she was working so hard to conceal that she was holding herself together by a very thin thread.

One of the hardest things he'd ever done was leaving her like that and walking out the door.

"Did you know he has a dog?"

"Leonard has a dog?" January asked, glancing up from her salad and meeting Helen's eyes. They were sharing a late lunch at January's desk. Helen had been recounting her previous night's date with Leonard.

"Oh, goodness no." Helen laughed around the folds of a paper napkin and carefully patted her mouth so that her lip gloss—the color, she'd informed January with a wicked grin, was Passionate Pumpkin—wouldn't smear. "Leonard can hardly take care of himself, let alone a dog. Michael. Michael has a dog. A big bushy hound named George. George the Bush. Get it? Don't ya just love it?"

January sighed and speared a crouton with her fork. It had been this way for over a week now. Since the night Michael had left her cowering like a whipped dog in the rain, he'd been dropping by the office to "chat" with Helen. Helen, in turn, never missed an opportunity to work some of her new found information about her "suitor elect" into conversations with January.

"His cat's name is Fluffy," Helen added.

January set aside her fork, fighting the picture that came to mind. Slowly removing her glasses, she studied Helen suspiciously. "Michael has a cat named Fluffy?"

"No, dear. Leonard. Leonard has a cat named Fluffy, though I can't for the life of me figure out why he gave it that name. Mangy critter has less hair than Leonard. I truly don't know why he keeps it around. Cats are so independent, they don't really need anyone to take care of them. Well, there, I guess I answered my own question, didn't I?" She giggled. Ignoring January's narrowed eyes, she busied herself stirring artificial sweetener into her tea and saturating her salad in French dressing. "Now a horse, there's an animal that requires a lot of care."

January sighed, regretting her question even as she asked it. "Who has a horse?"

Helen stared thoughtfully into space, her Sizzling Strawberry eye shadow giving her an otherworldly look. Finally she shrugged and said, "Oh, nobody I can think of, sweetie, but Michael could certainly have one if he wanted to. What with his family owning a cabin up in the mountains and all."

She'd had to reach quite a ways for that one, but January gave Helen credit. She was a craftsman. January felt like she was watching Helen piece together a patchwork quilt called The Life and Times of Michael Hayward. So now she knew that Michael had a dog and a cabin in the mountains. A couple more squares to add to the quilt Helen had been working on all week. January already knew far more about Michael Hayward than she wanted to. She knew enough to make him seem too human, too real . . . too nice.

She knew, for instance, that Michael owned a co-op apartment in New York City. Now that he was back in Boulder, though, he intended to sell the apartment and make Boulder his permanent residence. She also knew why he had gravitated to Boulder in the first place. Boulder was his birthplace. When she had met up with him fifteen years ago, he'd been living in Chicago. Evidently his work had taken him there, and since then it had taken him a little bit of everywhere. His family had remained settled in the Boulder area, and Michael, according to Helen, was a family-oriented man. His younger brother, Rob, was an engineer for the city development committee in nearby Longmont, and his sister, Gretchen, was married and lived in Boulder with her husband and two children. Finally, both of Michael's parents were retired and living in Denver. He wanted to be closer to all of them.

"Doesn't it sound romantic?" Helen's dreamy voice broke into January's thoughts. "A mountain retreat. Just imagine, moonlight on a fresh snowfall, a crackling fire in a huge stone hearth—"

"Helen . . ." January warned, but Helen went on like she hadn't heard.

"My Jack took me to a place like that for our honeymoon. It was one of the happiest times of my life."

The protest she was about to issue died on January's lips when she saw the faraway and poignant expression in Helen's eyes. Blinking hard, Helen met January's gaze. "You are blowing a very good thing here, sweetie."

January shook her head. "Helen, please—"

"January," Helen interrupted sternly, "I'm telling you, you are making the mistake of your life. This man is a special man. And despite the fact that you've done everything but kick him in the teeth, he keeps coming back. Do you have any idea what an unusual trait that is in a man as strong as he is? When are you going to get wise to the fact that he is no threat to you? That excuse he trumped up about wanting to do an article was only that, an excuse to find a way to meet you. All he wants from you is a chance to be with you."

January lost her appetite for her salad. "Helen, you know my reasons."

"Honey, I know. And I understand. But Jan, you

can't judge all men by your father. And you can't live your entire life through your work. It's not healthy. It's not even wise. You have so much courage. Show some of it now and take a chance on finding a little happiness, on having—heaven forbid—a little fun. Honey, you're entitled."

Entitled. That was a term January had never even vaguely associated with herself. Entitled. She rolled the thought around in her mind, but it drifted away in the wake of a still vivid, still terrifying childhood memory.

"Jan?"

She snapped her gaze to Helen's with a start.

"Honey, where were you? You looked like you were a million miles away."

January fought back unexpected threatening tears. She hadn't cried since she was a little girl. "I was," she said quietly. "I was a million miles away."

The sympathetic expression on Helen's face compelled January to confide something she'd never told another living soul. "My name was Elaine January Griffin," she said slowly. "Elaine, for my mother's sister. January, because my father took one look at me when I was born and said I was the spitting image of my mom. And since my mom was the coldest bitch he'd ever known, he wanted me named for the month that was as cold as she was." She thought of Michael comparing her kisses to cold beer and smiled tightly. "Some legacy, huh?"

"Oh, baby."

"What if I'm just like her, Helen?" She let the older woman see a weakness she'd never dared reveal, and it scared the hell out of her. "What if I can't respond to a man the way he needs a woman to respond to him? Maybe my father had a reason to drink. Maybe my mother's coldness drove him to it."

"And maybe your father's drinking was the reason your mother couldn't respond. In any event, you are *not* your mother. Despite everything you've been through, you're a warm, loving individual. Give yourself a chance to find out that you are also a warm, loving woman. Don't hide behind your fears any longer. Give Michael a chance."

She shook her head. "He scares me, Helen."

"Of course he does. He's the first man who's had a hide thick enough to take all the dirt you dish out and not tuck his tail between his legs and run away. Honey, you shouldn't let his persistence intimidate you. Let it lift you. He's one gorgeous hunk of man. Enjoy him."

"Enjoy him?"

"Yes, enjoy him. You do understand the term "enjoy," don't you? It's a bold new concept, I know, but rumor has it that it's catching on. Why, I understand some people actually work just five days a week now and take the other two days—I believe they call it a weekend—to relax and do fun things like date. Whoops, there's another new term for you. I'll explain—"

"Enough." January laughed. "I get the picture."

"We can only hope."

January smiled warmly. "You are a wild and wonderful woman." It was the closest she could come to an admission of love.

Helen flashed her a Cheshire cat grin. "So Leonard was saying last night."

As if on cue, the phone rang. Helen pounced on it.

"Good afternoon, January Stewart's office, how may I help you?" A wide, saucy grin split her face. "You make that request one more time, sweet thing, and I just might take you up on it."

January knew immediately that Michael was on the other end of the line. She felt her heart stutter, then slide into a deep, heavy cadence.

"How's my favorite flirt today?" Helen asked, then laughed wickedly. "I'll just bet you are." She giggled again, then listened. "January?" Helen raised a hopeful brow her way.

She came close, she really did, but in the end she couldn't make herself do it. Almost painfully, January shook her head.

Helen smiled sadly and turned back to the phone. "No, I'm sorry, Michael. She's not . . ." Helen paused, then finally finished, ". . . available. No, I couldn't say when. What? Oh, sure. I'll give her the message. You, too, you big rascal."

She hung up and said flatly, "Michael says hello."

January fixed her concentration on the cherry tomato she'd been chasing around her salad bowl for the past five minutes and waited for the lecture she knew would follow. It didn't come. Instead, Helen gathered the remains of her lunch and, clucking like a chicken, flapped her way out of the room.

January tossed her salad in the trash and crossed her arms over her breasts. "I'm not chicken!" she shouted above Helen's noisy exit. "I'm just cautious. Is there any crime in that?"

Helen responded with several shrill, insistent clucks.

January grinned in spite of her irritation. "As long as you're in the mood," she yelled, "I could use a dozen eggs."

Four

January liked autumn best. The colors, the scents, the clean, crisp zip in the air. She shoved the sleeves of her heavy gray sweat shirt up to her elbows and dug a little harder for the run up the hill. By the time she reached the summit she was gasping for air and clutching her aching sides. She'd pushed too hard—nothing new—and now she had to pay the piper.

Veering off the jogging path at a slow, cool-down trot, she ducked under some low-hanging branches and followed a little-used trail through the thickest part of the woods, heading toward the creek. This time of day, early on a Saturday morning and in full sunlight, she didn't worry about the isolation and the vulnerability of a woman alone. She welcomed the solitude and the peace that came with it.

When she reached the creek, she sat down on the carpet of dried maple and aspen leaves and listened to the gurgle of water tripping over the stony creek bed. Slowly her breathing returned to normal and the ache eased out of her side.

Complacent in a way that only the afterburn of

physical exertion could make her, she flopped down on her back and indulged in some rare and basic laziness. Feeling like a kid playing hooky, she watched through the lacework of bare tree limbs as china white clouds cruised against the backdrop of the blue Colorado sky.

And she thought of Michael.

Michael, and the way he'd tasted when he kissed her the night he'd brought her home in the rain. Michael, and the way he'd caressed her with his eyes and made her insides go all zingy and weak. Michael, and the way he'd looked like a little boy lost when she'd slammed the door in his face. She flinched just thinking about what she'd done to him, then felt a hollow ache of guilt remembering the anguish in his eyes when he'd realized she had prepared herself for a blow.

She still didn't know where that reaction had come from. She'd known he wouldn't physically hurt her, but another kind of fear had muddled things up. She was afraid she was beginning to care about him. The emotions he stirred inside her were so powerful, yet the memories he brought with him were so painful.

How could one man represent both threat and promise? He made her feel as out of control as runaway fireworks on the Fourth of July. She'd never known a man who had the power to dominate her thoughts this way, who made her consider her personal priorities over her professional ones. The children had always come first, and yet now, because of Michael, she wanted that number one spot for herself.

Pulling her knees up until they were pointing skyward, she flung an arm over her eyes and tried to analyze why she reacted to him that way.

The only thing she ended up analyzing was how he'd looked in those biker boots and bun-hugging jeans, then in banker flannel and a crisply knotted tie. She groaned and became so lost in the tummy-tightening images, it was a moment before she realized she was no longer alone.

She sat up, alert to the brittle snap of dry tree limbs and the crunch of running footsteps over fallen leaves and pine needles. Before she had a chance to register alarm or had the presence of mind to rise to her feet, two huge, furry paws hit her full in the chest and shoved her to her back again.

"Dammit, George! Come back here!"

With a disjointed sense of relief, she recognized his voice. Michael was clearly irritated, and his curse rose above the deep-throated barking of what appeared to be one hundred pounds of dog in a teddy bear suit.

Ignoring his master, the bushy critter pinned her to the ground and exuberantly washed every inch of her face with a huge, pink tongue.

"Get off her, you big oaf!"

As fast as her canine admirer had arrived, he was gone, not of his own volition, but because Michael had forcefully dragged him away. Still battling the excited dog, Michael knelt by her side.

"January?" He had the audacity to look surprised when he realized it was her. "Oh, Lord, January. Are you all right?"

"I'm fine." She sat up slowly. "But as approaches go, I've got to tell you, this one lacks your usual finesse."

He grinned sheepishly. "Yeah, well, what George lacks in finesse, he makes up for in sheer animal magnetism. Not that it'll cut any weight right now, but you should feel honored that he attacked you. He only does that to people he truly likes."

"Likes?" Charmed but not wanting to be, she

gave George a forgiving scratch under his chin. "As in affection, or as in for dinner?"

Michael's grin became a full-fledged smile. "As in affection. Our taste in ladies is very similar."

It struck January then that she didn't want to be angry at Michael for invading her solitude. Once she accepted that, it was less difficult to admit that she was glad to see him. From the look in his eyes and the sudden quiet between them, it would seem he, too, sensed the change in her attitude.

Apparently he didn't quite know how to react to it either, because he busied himself with quick, absent pats to George's back. "If you can behave," he said finally, directing his comment to George, "I'll let you go play."

George's response was an enthusiastic attempt to peel the skin off Michael's face with one huge, scraping stroke of his tongue.

"Where's the squirrel, George?" Michael asked in staged excitement. George bounced up and down like a little kid looking for Santa. "Go get him! Go get the squirrel."

George charged away, his nose to the ground, searching diligently for a scent.

Michael grinned. "Works every time. It should keep him busy and out of your hair for a while."

Feeling suddenly like their chaperon had exited stage left, January tried to direct her attention toward the creek and away from Michael. Tried and failed. Without her permission, her gaze strayed back to his devastating smile.

She looked at him uncertainly, telling herself there wasn't a reason in the world for her to find him so attractive today. Gone were both the biker and the businessman. In their place was a reject from a soup kitchen.

Knotted string and athletic tape held a pair of grungy jogging shoes together. His dingy gray sweat pants had holes in both knees, and the sweat shirt that used to boast the letters U.S.C. but now showed just an outline, was frayed at the neck. The sleeves appeared to have been chewed off just above his elbows. A crimson sweatband held his unruly black hair away from his face and provided the only splash of color, except, of course, for the multifaceted diamond that glittered intriguingly in his left ear.

Not exactly the stuff dreams are made of, she thought, and not exactly a threat, either. "Nice outfit, Hayward. What'd you do, roll a bum on the way over and swipe his clothes?"

He pretended to scowl. "This from a woman with leaves in her hair and paw prints on her . . . ummm, shirt."

She looked down, felt herself redden, then brushed self-consciously at the dark marks imprinted over each breast.

When she raised her eyes, Michael was sitting back on his heels, studying her as if trying to gauge her mood. "I don't suppose," he began as he gently tugged a leaf from her hair, "that it would do any good to tell you it really is an accident that George and I stumbled on to you today."

Something in his expression made her want to believe him. A long nurtured resistance to trust, however, wouldn't let her. "It does seem a little strange that I've never seen you here before."

He shifted his weight until he was sitting beside her. Linking his wrists over upraised knees, he looked speculatively at her. "You mean you run here often?"

Seeing his genuine surprise, she realized he was telling the truth. "Not as often as I should," she admitted, feeling an unsolicited sting of disappointment that their meeting was coincidental. Afraid he'd read her thoughts through her eyes, she diverted her gaze to the creek. "I rarely stray off the main path. But it's so pretty up here, I couldn't resist today."

"It is pretty," he agreed. "This is George's favorite spot in the park. I think he pretends he's a frontier dog making the wilderness safe for new settlers."

His silly banter eased the tension that had been building and drew a laugh from her. It bubbled out, quick and unguarded, as she watched the huge, lumbering dog crash about in his quest for the elusive and bloodthirsty squirrel.

Michael became very quiet. With a soft smile still lingering on her mouth, she met his eyes. The heat she saw shimmering there made her breath catch.

"Definitely worth the wait," he murmured.

Her questioning frown brought a quick, heart-melting explanation.

"Since the first time I saw you, I've been wanting to make you smile." He touched a finger gently, lightly, to the corner of her mouth. "It was nice," he said in a hoarse whisper. "Very, very nice."

The wanting revealed in his eyes was eloquent in its intensity and frightening in its implication. Afraid to acknowledge that mixed with that hunger was a kindness, a caring, and an unexpected vulnerability that touched her bone-deep, she quickly looked away.

She could feel his gaze still touching her, and tried not to think about the fact that she wore absolutely no makeup, that in all likelihood her hair rivaled Helen's in the wild mop department, and that she had a huge, grubby paw print stamped over each breast.

Michael shared her quiet for a long moment before he rose slowly to his feet.

"Well, George and I have intruded long enough." He gestured vaguely toward her shirt. "Sorry about that. If he did any permanent damage, ah, to the shirt, I mean, let me know, and I'll replace it."

If she didn't know better, she'd think he was flustered. And somehow, a flustered Michael Hayward was much less threatening . . . and achingly more appealing.

"It's no problem, really." She shrugged dismissively and felt her heart kick her a couple of good ones in the chest. He was leaving. Without her request, he was going to leave her alone.

Helen's words came back to haunt her: *You are blowing a very good thing here, sweetie.* She swallowed hard, knowing that if she didn't say or do something, he'd be gone. And she didn't want him to go.

Maybe it was the moon. Maybe it was just a temporary lapse in sanity. Or maybe she was simply tired of fighting the feelings. Whatever it was, it had taken over, because she heard herself say his name. "Michael . . ."

His look was expectant, yet cautious, when he turned back to her, a panting George in tow.

She rose slowly, brushing off her bottom as she straightened. "I—I know it was a long time ago that you offered," she said haltingly, "but, about that dinner invitation. If—if it's still open . . ."

Had she said that? she wondered. Had those words actually come out of her mouth?

The dark light in his eyes told her he was as surprised as she was. "It's still open, Counselor. You just name the time."

How about next year? she thought, her courage slinking away. She licked her suddenly dry lips. "Next Saturday?"

His smile was slow, pleased, and steady. "Seven o'clock?"

Lacking the will or the desire to stop herself, she

nodded. It was done. An irrevocable, irretrievable step in the wrong direction.

He returned her nod, corralled George, and with a wink and a wave, disappeared through the thickest part of the woods.

She was alone again . . . with her hammering heart, with her better judgment shattered, and, in the wake of what she sensed was a colossal mistake, with a smile she couldn't control or explain.

As is often the way of things, January compounded her mistake with another. Monday morning she told Helen about the dinner date.

Helen's response was a rebel yell that would have inspired the Yanks to surrender to the Rebs at Vicksburg. When the windows quit rattling, she offered to make January an appointment with her hairdresser, then insisted on taking her shopping for a dress that would, in her words, "tighten his shorts but good."

With images of frizzy pink hair fueling her argument, January skirted the issue of Helen's beautician by promising to make an appointment with her own. The shopping trip, however, was not open to debate.

"Leonard's been talking cruise for a couple of weeks now," Helen said exuberantly. "You can help me shop for some sun clothes, and I'll help you pick out a dress."

So after work that evening, January found herself in a chic boutique, trying on a classy black sheath.

"Oh, sweetie," Helen said when January emerged from the dressing room. "Look at you. You've got breasts! Nice big ones. Who'd have guessed it?"

"Helen," January warned when a salesclerk floated by, arching a censoring brow.

"Well," Helen muttered, and toned her comments down to a loud whisper. "All I ever see you in are those stuffy suits. Lordy, lordy," she continued after a second prideful appraisal. "If you aren't a sight!"

"You don't think it's too much?" January asked, checking out all the angles in the three-way mirror. She had to admit, the dress was flattering. Though black and basic, the cut and style were feminine and chic, from the off-the-shoulder neckline and long, tight sleeves, to the tightly nipped-in waist and the short, slim skirt that ended a few inches above her knees.

"Oh, it's too much, all right," Helen said. "So much, in fact, that I'm going to worry more about Michael than I am about you. The man doesn't have a prayer." She giggled. "Not an amen. Not a hallelujah!"

"In spite of your enthusiasm," January said dryly, "I think I'll buy it."

She also ended up buying a pair of black heels with straps to go with it.

An hour later it was Helen's turn to model sun clothes.

"Well, what do you think?" Helen asked, smiling expectantly as she emerged from the dressing room wearing knee-high hose, heels, and a chartreuse and purple floral swimsuit with a plunging neckline and a ruffled skirt.

It was all January could do to keep her jaw off the floor. "It's . . . it's . . ."

"A stunner, huh?" Helen said brightly.

Over a bottle of wine several years ago, Helen had confided to January that she lived in horror of becoming a dull, blue-haired little old lady. Loving her for fighting that fear, January smiled broadly. "That's the word all right."

• • •

Six-thirty Saturday night found January calm, collected, and in complete control. At least that was the appearance the woman in her dressing table mirror projected.

With robotlike motions, she dabbed perfume behind each ear. Untying her robe, she applied the same scent between her breasts, then, after a moment's hesitation, to the insides of her thighs. She stood stiffly and slipped out of her robe. As she stared stonily at the body she'd soaked and oiled like a sacrificial offering, she reaffirmed what she planned to do.

Living in a constant state of quandary was Helen's style, not hers. So she'd pulled herself together and reached a decision midweek. No man was worth the mental anguish she'd put herself through since the day she'd succumbed to the charm of a bushy brown dog named George and his outlaw owner.

Therefore, January no longer looked upon the evening to come as a date, but rather as a life experience she'd put off too long. It was time to find out what all the fuss was about.

Michael was a player. He played at life, he played at loving. And he played the game well. Why he'd decided she was someone he wanted to play with, she wasn't quite sure. She strongly suspected, however, that despite his single-minded attempt at seduction, once he'd won, he'd be ready to move on to a new sport.

If it hurt a little to accept that, it was the price she paid for giving in to his charm. But she'd also decided that since she was going to be a participant in this event, she was going to reap a few of the rewards as well. She was a twenty-eight-year-old virgin. A dirigible in the jet age. What better man to choose for her first lover than the wise and worldly Michael Hayward?

Besides, she'd come to believe Helen was right. Evading Michael wasn't the answer. He was by nature an investigator, and although he'd quit pushing about the article, she was convinced that if she continued to elude him, he'd start digging into her past until he found out everything he wanted to know. It wasn't worth the risk. The sooner she got him out of her life, the better. And as soon as he found out about her inexperience, he'd get bored and be gone.

She turned stoically to the underthings she'd laid out with surgical precision on her bed—Helen's gifts for her date.

"You can't wear white cotton panties beneath a dress that shouts black lace, sweetie," Helen had said, and shoved the box of goodies into January's hands. "It just wouldn't do."

Looking at the "goodies" now, January decided they'd look great on a model smiling provocatively from the glossy pages of a men's magazine, inviting the reader to: "Dial a date, darlin'."

Determined to see this through, she picked up the lacy black garter belt, swallowed hard, and slipped it up and over her bare hips. Careful to keep the seams straight, she eased into the sheer black stockings and inexpertly fastened them front and back. The black lace camisole came next, squeezing snugly across her ribs and cupping her breasts so that they spilled over the top of the underwire bra cups. Last were the tap pants. Indulging, just a little, in the fantasy, she watched in the mirror as she stepped into the soft, silky garment. Uninvited, a sensual, sultry picture developed of Michael slipping them back off with great pleasure.

She shivered despite a sudden heat that ignited

in her breast and radiated through her body like a slow-moving flame. The delicious warmth surprised her . . . and frightened her. She wasn't prepared for the force of it. Or for the anticipation of how this evening would end.

A glance at her bedside clock confirmed that Michael would be there any minute. She carefully removed the black dress from its padded hanger and slipped into it and her heels. A lengthy appraisal in the mirror told her that the gold ear bobs and matching choker Helen had loaned her were a stunning complement to the dress.

The ringing of the doorbell told her she wasn't as ready for this as she'd thought.

Her first inclination was to walk directly into the closet, shut the door behind her, and stay there until he went away. In the end, the mental image of the tongue-lashing she'd get from Helen if she took the coward's way out was what coaxed her out of the bedroom.

Like a prisoner heading down death row, she went to answer the door.

Michael had reached a decision midweek. The lady didn't know it yet, he thought as he waited for her to answer the door, but she needed him. He could see it in her eyes every time she let herself look at him, could see a raw, aching loneliness. A hunger. Not just a physical hunger, but the soul-deep, heart-knotting hunger a good woman feels for a good man. He wanted to be that man. He wanted to feed that hunger. But if he scared her off before she understood how good he was for her, she'd bolt again, and he'd have no one to blame but himself. And they'd both be losers.

So his word for the day was cool. He'd been cool when his contact from Denver had called to tell him he still hadn't had any luck tracking down a history on January Stewart. He'd been cool when he'd come home from a quick trip to the dry cleaners to find that George had eaten his favorite racquetball racket. And he was going to be cool tonight and keep his hands to himself if he had to kick himself in the shins to do it.

But when January opened her door and gave him that long, slow blink that was sexier than any blatant come-on he'd ever fielded, cool flew out the window and he damn near went up in flames.

"Hi," she said, her husky voice revealing her nervousness.

"Hi, yourself," he managed to say, and, regaining a small measure of his presence of mind, added a hoarse, "You look sensational."

She looked absolutely edible! She'd whipped her hair into a soft, sassy froth of curls that showcased her delicate features, emphasizing her aristocratic cheekbones and her pert little nose. Her eyes seemed as black as the dress she was wearing, a dress that was designed, he was sure, to make a man fantasize about the feel of the soft, full breasts beneath it, and the endless, *endless* length of legs disappearing above the hem of the skirt.

She smiled self-consciously and stepped back from the door. "Please, come in."

Slipping inside and closing the door behind him, Michael extended a gaily wrapped package. "This is from George," he said. Chucking his edict to keep his hands to himself, he tugged her slowly but forcefully toward him. "And this," he whispered, lowering his head, "is from me."

The eyes that looked questioningly into his were startled but not afraid. Promising himself he'd do nothing to reignite her fear, he touched his mouth to hers with a feather-light pressure. When she didn't resist, when in fact, she hesitantly slipped her arms around his waist, he felt something akin to an explosion rumble through his chest. The aftershocks spread at the speed of light to every extremity of his body. With a groan, he pulled her tighter against him and deepened the kiss.

Her lips softened, then parted beneath his, with an arresting innocence. He felt a sensual urgency in the way she cautiously accepted the first touch of his tongue, the first deep stroke.

Shaken by the intensity of his physical reactions and by the speed with which she'd aroused him, he lifted his head and set her a step away before he lost complete control.

Clearing his throat, he gazed into her slightly dazed eyes and spoke with a lightness he was far from feeling.

"George's feelings will be hurt if you don't open that."

For a moment she looked confused, then remembered the package in her hand. "Oh . . . oh, Michael, really, this isn't necessary."

He held out his hands, palms up. "I told him that, but he insisted. Go ahead. Open it."

With a wary but pleased little smile, she carefully unwrapped the package. A swift and strong flash of insight told him she wasn't used to receiving presents. He was still analyzing that impression and deciding how he was going to rectify it when she pulled out the pale pink sweat shirt. She sliced him a puzzled look before studying the logo on the front of the shirt. A huge, comically daffy dog grinned back at her. The dog, bearing an uncanny resemblance to George, was wearing his own sweat shirt which boasted the words: "I brake for trees" in big black letters.

Michael watched her eyes light up in totally spontaneous, totally unguarded amusement, and he decided it would be a good idea for him to make love to her right then and there. It might just teach her that it's not nice to mess with a man's cool with a smile that generated megawatts of crackling sensual heat.

Reluctantly, he controlled his urges. "I told him it was silly," he said, "that if he really wanted to square things with you he should have sent flowers or candy, but he insisted you'd look pretty in pink."

"You tell George," she said as she avoided meeting his eyes and worked overhard in placing the shirt back in the box, "that it's a very special gift, and I like it better than any flowers or candy he could have sent me." After sending him a brief look of thanks, she excused herself to get her purse.

Michael took advantage of her absence to cool himself down and to familiarize himself with her home. The one and only time he'd been inside, he'd been too angry and then too stunned to appreciate what she'd done to convert a modest, predictable suburban cottage into a unique, stylish home.

His little lawyer loved color. He wasn't surprised about that, or that he'd started thinking of her as his little anything. Somehow he'd known that beneath all those stoic power suits of navy and gray, she had a passion for pretty things. For some reason, though, she seemed to think she didn't dare let anyone know it. But at home, on her own turf, she could use whatever splashes of color she chose, and she chose well. From the dramatic jade and silver in her foyer, to the southwestern pastels in her living room, he was impressed with her sense of taste and style. Just thinking about what she might have done in her bedroom had his head spinning.

Yet this was no decorator's layout of clinical perfection. Michael felt a certain warmth, a certain love, that no professional could have achieved in January's eclectic mix of old and new, bargain basement and home crafted. And everywhere, everywhere, were thriving green plants.

He'd just made out the initials on a particularly stunning watercolor when he heard her come back into the living room. "You did this?" he asked over his shoulder as she walked up behind him.

She nodded.

He moved to study the other pieces around the room. "You did all of these," he said, impressed. "They're wonderful."

She shrugged off the compliment. "I minored in art prior to law school. It's still an outlet for me."

It was the first piece of information about her private self that she'd ever offered voluntarily. He felt like she'd dropped a big fat piece of pie in his lap. He loved pie. He was going to love cracking the protective armor on this lady even more.

Sensing, however, that now was not the time to push with questions, he helped her on with her coat. "I hope you like the Flagstaff House."

"I've never been there."

"Then, dear lady, prepare to be pampered, placated, and pleasured with one of the finest dining experiences of your life."

"That nice?"

"Oh, yeah, it's nice, but I was talking about my company."

He raised his eyebrows suggestively and was rewarded with another unguarded smile. He could get used to those smiles. He *planned* on getting used to them.

But nothing ever went according to his plans. Not where January was concerned.

He'd intended to wine and dine her out of enough personal information to fill a couple of volumes. Instead, by the time the dessert had been served to top off their five course meal, *he* was the one who'd done all of the talking. The enchanting little witch had managed to make him spill his guts.

She now knew everything about him from his shoe size to his shorts size and some embarrassing childhood stories in between. A two-hour dining experience, for pity's sake, he thought, and the sum total of the new information he'd discovered on the elusive Ms. Stewart was what he'd picked up before they'd left her house. She'd pay for that, he decided as he helped her out of his Mercedes in front of her house. She'd pay good.

He knew her game. He'd sensed her withdraw into herself on the drive home. The fear was taking over again. He could feel it. She would let him walk her to the door, offer a chaste good-night kiss, and send him home to a cold shower.

Well, he had a surprise for her. He was going to kiss her senseless as punishment for making him sing like a snitch in an Elmore Leonard novel. Then he was going to leave her with her own fire burning and let her figure out how to put it out. That would fix her.

He hadn't yet made his move when she very quietly, very nervously asked, "Would you like to come in?"

He was so stunned by her invitation, he didn't remember replying. He must have, though, because the next thing he knew, he was standing inside her foyer and she was hanging up his coat.

"I had a wonderful time tonight," she said breathlessly as she turned back to him.

"Yes. It was nice, wasn't it?" he heard himself respond in a voice that sounded like he'd just swallowed a mouthful of tacks.

Watching her carefully, he saw her draw in a deep breath, raise her chin, and lick the last of the gloss off her lips. That innocent gesture rocked him all the way to his toes . . . and to other places he was trying desperately not to think about.

"I—I was hoping," she went on hesitantly, "that . . . maybe it didn't have to end just yet."

He was sure he'd only imagined what she'd said, and chalked it off to delusional hysteria. But when he met her eyes and saw a glimmer of hope—or was it apprehension?—flash through their beautiful dark depths, he knew he'd heard her right. He knew what she was offering.

It was all he'd hoped for. It was all he'd fantasized about for weeks.

And it was all wrong.

He wasn't sure why, but he knew it was wrong.

With a pinched little smile, she reached for his hand. Hers was trembling as she led him down the hall to her bedroom.

She flipped on the light and left him frowning in the doorway as she walked to her closet, then removed her heels and hung them neatly on a shoe rack. Peripherally aware of a white upon white decor, from the carpet to the drapes to the bedspread on the old brass bed, he watched her in a dazed state, trying to figure out what was wrong with this picture.

"January—" he began, but stopped abruptly when she crossed the room to him, presented her back, and in a small, controlled voice asked, "Could you get this for me?"

A man could only take so much. Intoxicated by her bold maneuver and by the scent that had been driving him crazy all night, he reached for the tab of her zipper, and, enjoying every pale, cool inch of flesh he revealed, slid the zipper down.

Like an automaton, she slipped the dress off her shoulders and stepped out of it. He'd seen black lace and silk stockings before, but he'd never seen them on January. He swallowed hard and felt his testosterone level hit a new high.

He'd been wrong earlier. Her legs weren't endless. They were all pale satin skin and firm supple flesh, and they ended at the exact spot he wanted to touch and taste and claim as belonging only to him.

She was exquisite, every man's erotic dream. And she was his for the taking.

He whispered her name as he spun her around and hauled her hard against him. He would have been aghast at his own lack of finesse if he hadn't been so lost in the wildfire her mouth ignited.

When the kiss ended, he was reeling and already working at the knot of his tie. Yet as he watched her walk calmly back to the closet, where she proceeded to hang up her dress and tuck it carefully into a garment bag, it hit him what was going on.

What he was going to do about it was a measure of how far gone he was on this woman. He cursed under his breath, closed his eyes, and kissed sweet relief good-bye.

Five

January counted to ten, drew a shaky breath, and closed the closet door. She didn't have to look at Michael to know he was watching her every move. His bold, silent shadow filled her bedroom doorway. The heat from his eyes seemed to touch every pulse point, every inch of skin she'd so brazenly revealed.

She didn't feel so brazen right now. She felt exposed and vulnerable as she crossed silently to her bed—her lily white virgin's bed that had never held a man's weight, had never taken a lover into its waiting warmth.

Resolved to see this through to the end, she turned back the bedspread with a trembling hand, silently damning Michael for not helping her. He'd picked a fine time to play the hesitant suitor. Why was he just standing there? Her plan had only extended as far as getting him to her bedroom. He was supposed to pick up the action from there. *He* was the one with the experience, the one who'd been forcing this issue all along. Where was that cocky, exasperating flirt when she needed him?

With a determination fostered by the last of her bravery, she turned to face him.

Still he waited just inside the door.

Her heart tripped clumsily, then slammed against her chest. "Michael?" She paused, gathering her courage once more. "Aren't you coming?"

His eyes darkened before he dropped his chin to his chest and expelled a deep, weary breath. A soft, self-mocking chuckle escaped him as he looked back up at her and shook his head. "Not tonight, January. Much as he regrets it, Mr. Hayward will not be coming tonight."

She blinked as his deliberately crude meaning registered. She understood rejection; she'd grown up with it. This was rejection at its elemental best.

A stunning rush of mortification ripped fresh wounds inside her. The accompanying pain cut that much deeper because she had no one to blame but herself.

She didn't know what to say. She only knew what she wanted to do—disappear. Find a deep, dark hole and crawl into it.

Feeling like she'd been physically beaten, she walked on shaking legs to the closet and reached for her bathrobe. A strong hand grasped her arm, intercepting her.

"Let's get something straight here, Counselor," Michael said, turning her toward him. "I won't be making love with you tonight, but it's *not* because I don't want to." His gaze was fierce and unrelenting as it dropped to her mouth and lingered there before climbing slowly back to her eyes. "Make no mistake about it. I want you. I've wanted you from the first time I saw you."

Confused and still reeling from the pain of his rejection, she tried to pull away. With little effort, he folded her tightly in his arms. "If you can't make yourself believe what you hear, believe what you feel." He hauled her flush against him, aligning his hips with hers.

She sucked in a harsh breath when she felt the hot, thick length of his arousal press against her belly. Then she felt him shudder, felt his slow bold caress as he kneaded her buttocks through thin silk until, as if he couldn't help himself, his hands tunneled up under the legs of her tap pants.

"Michael!" She gasped and stiffened as he filled his palms with her bare flesh.

"Shhh." He buried his face in her hair. "Just feel the heat, January. Do you feel it?"

She felt a fire! Not that low, slow, licking flame that had drifted through her blood the first time she'd looked into his eyes, but a wild, rampaging inferno ignited by the fit of his body to hers, by the crush of his hands on her skin.

Despite her attempt to fight it, a desperate yearning swamped her. She felt her resistance melt, her body relax and lean into his of its own will. Lifting her hands to his shoulders, she clung to his solid strength—only to have him grip her waist and set her firmly away.

"No, babe. This is not going to happen tonight."

Rejection slammed back full force. Whatever his game was, he'd gone too far. Out of sheer defiant pride, she kept her voice from trembling. "I think you'd better leave."

"I'm not going anywhere until we talk."

"I don't have anything to say to you."

"Oh, but you do," he assured her as he snagged her robe and tossed it to her.

She clutched the white terry cloth to her breast and glared at him.

"Put it on."

"Get out."

"Not a chance. Not until you tell me what tonight was all about."

"Tonight," she began, shrugging jerkily into the robe and cinching the belt tight, "was obviously a mistake."

"Why? Because I didn't end up in your bed?"

She met his insult with her chin held high. "Because I was a fool to think I wanted you there."

"You wanted me there? Why?" he asked softly. "I asked you why, January. Why did you think you wanted me in your bed?"

At that moment, she couldn't imagine why. She hated him! She hated herself more for having forgotten, even for a moment, what a bastard he was, what he'd done to her all those years ago.

"Okay," he said reasonably when she refused to answer. "Let me tell you why. But first, let's get a few things out in the open." He walked to the bed, propped both pillows against the brass headrail, and turned to her. "You might as well get comfortable because this may take a while."

She was no match for him physically, January thought. If he'd decided he was going to stay, she couldn't make him leave. Resigned to that fact, she walked stiffly across the room and plopped down on the bed. The sooner she did as he asked, the sooner he'd be gone.

He sat beside her, facing her, forcing her to scooch her hips over to make room. Leaning back against the pillows, she wrapped her robe around her legs and drew them to her chest.

"You don't have to take a protective posture with me, January. It's never been my intent to hurt you. But you don't buy that, do you? I'm not talking about physically hurting you. If there's one thing I'm sure of, it's that you know I'd never lay a hand on you in anger. But there's something else, isn't there? For some reason, you have always been sure I represent a threat to you. Someday I'll find out why. Someday you're going to trust me enough to tell me. And someday I'll make you believe that whatever it is you're afraid of could never happen."

Before she could fully digest the implication of "someday" and the panic his softly but firmly posed promise incited, he began again.

"I've been up-front with you since day one, lady. Well . . ." He shrugged and amended, "Maybe not from the first day. But that was because I didn't know how deep I was into this until you threw me out on my ear. It hadn't occurred to me that you might not feel the same spark I did. And when you made it clear you didn't want to see me again, I realized I just couldn't let that happen."

She tried to look bored, but she was hanging on his every word, even as she loathed herself for listening. Plucking absently at the bed sheet, she avoided looking him in the eye.

The touch of his hand on her cheek brought her head up.

"You're a virgin, aren't you?" he asked, gently tucking a runaway fall of hair behind her ear.

If he'd said the house was on fire, he would have surprised her less. She felt her eyes widen reflectively, felt the heat of a thousand candles flood her cheeks with embarrassment.

Leaning toward her, he placed a soft, chaste kiss on her forehead, then rested his hand on her updrawn knee. "I think it's beautiful," he whispered. "I think you're beautiful.

"It took a while for me to piece together what was going on," he continued, caressing her leg through the heavy robe. "But finally I realized that nothing about tonight added up. You've been avoiding me for weeks, then out of the blue we have a dinner date. That should have been my first clue. That abrupt little turnaround without so much as a phone call or lunch between us.

"But it was the little things that finally gave you

away, like the way you jump whenever I touch you. The way you stiffen then force yourself to relax before you let yourself enjoy a kiss. Look at me, January."

His voice was soft and compelling. When she did as he asked, he smiled kindly. "Honey, a woman in the throes of passion simply doesn't spend ten minutes hanging up a dress that should have been left in a puddle on the floor."

Beyond humiliation, she linked her arms around her knees and buried her face between them.

He squeezed her leg and continued in that same consoling voice. "What you were going to pull on me tonight was a dirty, low-down trick. Not that I don't appreciate the motive, but I won't be used. I won't be your experiment, or a convenient vehicle to get this little biological embarrassment out of the way. That's what you'd decided, hadn't you? If I was going to make such a pest of myself, you might as well get a little something out of the deal too. I'm right, aren't I? Aren't I?"

Her silence rang like a self-indictment.

"I'm sorry, baby, but it just won't work that way. Don't get me wrong. I intend to make love with you."

Her head came up at that.

"Make love," he repeated with feeling. "Not take you to bed, not have sex with you. Make love with you. Do you understand what I'm telling you?"

When she started to lower her head again, he stayed her with a hand under her jaw. "I forgive you for planning to use me. I even admire the courage it took to make the decision and follow through with it, when the very idea obviously scared you to death. But until you confide in me about what frightens you, until I feel you're ready to make love and not just have sex, it's not going to happen between us no matter how much I want it to."

The hand that held her jaw slid down to her throat. His thumb stroked her skin in a slow, tender caress. "I need commitment here, January. I need some mutual trust, some honest caring. And even if it kills me, I'll have it before I ever have you. What I feel for you is special and new to me. I'm not yet sure what it all means, but I know I won't jeopardize what it might become by pushing you into something when you're just not ready."

January was too stunned to speak, too rattled by his declaration to absorb all the words he had spoken. Words like commitment, and trust, and caring. They were foreign and frightening, and they got all tangled up with her insecurity and the strange and uninvited warmth his promises implied.

"Consider this fair warning, Counselor. I intend to make you ready for whatever is intended to happen between us. You haven't seen the last of me. Not by a long shot. And I haven't seen nearly enough of you."

His gaze still locked with hers, he lowered his hands to her waist. "Starting with tonight. You're going to get used to me touching you, looking at you. Wanting you." His fingers poised at the knotted belt. "Let me?"

Inside her head, that old censoring voice screamed a resounding, *No!* But a new, needy voice whispered back his words like a litany . . . trust, commitment, caring. And Lord help her, she wanted to believe them.

She closed her eyes and let her head fall back against the pillows.

When he opened the robe, she didn't stop him. When he slipped it one torturous inch at a time from her shoulders, reason, like sanity, slipped right along with it.

"You're trembling," he said in a gruff whisper. "I

want you to tremble, but not because you're afraid. I want you to shiver, but not from cold."

She was anything but cold. She was on fire.

"Open your eyes, Counselor. Look at me when I touch you."

She swallowed hard and did his bidding. His eyes were so open, so beseeching, so breathtakingly blue as he touched a hand to her throat where her pulse hammered wildly.

"This is where the trust comes in. Kiss me, January." He urged her gently toward him. "Kiss me because you want to. Because it feels good."

His whispered request nurtured a thrilling need to grow to aching proportions within her. But even as the featherlight warmth of his breath against her mouth stirred the woman in her to a ripe awareness, an old and long-standing fear made her hesitate. "Michael—"

"Shhh. I know. You hadn't planned to have to think about this, had you? It's scary, but it's only a kiss. Just a kiss. That's all I want. You set the tone, you set the pace. Don't think past that. Just take it one step at a time. We'll get into the really scary stuff later."

Stuff like commitment and trust and caring, she thought as those words again rattled around in her head like old bones. Deep down it was those words, not his touch, that scared her the most. His touch was somehow reassuring, something tangible and real amid the swirl of contradicting messages her brain was sending to her body.

"Please?" she heard him whisper.

"I . . . I'm not very good at this," she mumbled finally.

He smiled. "Let me be the judge of that."

It was his smile that finally did it, the openness of it, his wanting so thinly veiled.

Ever so slowly she leaned forward. Closing her

eyes she pressed her mouth to his once, gently. Then again with less hesitancy, because she couldn't quite believe his lips were as firm yet as yielding as she'd first thought them to be. And because he was keeping his promise and letting her set the pace, she kissed him a third time.

By now she was fascinated by the taste of him, the heat, the intriguing scent that was unique to him. It made her think of exotic spice and old leather . . . and of dark silken shadows and the heat of a softly flickering candle.

She kissed him once more and, touching her fingers to his face, explored the slightly abrasive stubble that darkened his impossibly masculine jaw.

His deep, throaty groan loosed a rich and melting warmth that sluiced through her thickening blood. When he trembled as if he, too, were struggling for control, a stunning sensual awakening swept her from breast to belly, stealing her hesitancy.

Emboldened by his reactions, she experimented with the first shy touch of her tongue to his lips. He stiffened as if his body were one tightly clenched fist, and she felt the electrifying evidence of a woman's power.

Wide-eyed, she drew away.

"Trust me," he said hoarsely, visibly working to pull himself together. "You are very, very good at this."

She felt a flood of color stain her cheeks.

"Too good to give up on," he added. "Too much to walk away from." His eyes had gone smoky with passion, yet he met her gaze steadily. "Prepare yourself to be wooed, Counselor. Yes, wooed." He chuckled at her dazed frown. "I'm going to court you and spoil you and worm my charming little self into your heart until you can't imagine what life would be without me. I know." He intercepted her protest with two gentle fingers on her lips. "Your calendar is full. Let me worry about that. I'll make room."

"Michael—"

"Have you noticed yet that you really don't have much to say about this?"

She nodded, wrestling with the beginning of a grin.

"Smart girl. Now don't fight it. Just come along for the ride. Will you give me that much, January?"

"You just told me I didn't have a choice."

"See what a fast study you are?"

"Michael—"

"Shhh. I've got to go while I still have the strength to leave you."

She blinked, a slow, languorous reaction to the desire shining in his eyes.

He groaned. "Lord, woman, don't do that." His mood changed suddenly from playful to pensive as his gaze, dark and cloudy again, roamed restlessly over her face before dropping to the black lace that, by design, revealed far more than it concealed.

She tensed all over as his rapt attention lingered on her breasts, then descended to her thighs. With infinite care, his hand followed.

She shuddered as he cupped her breast through the lace, then moaned as, with just the brush of his thumb over her nipple, brought it to a tight, pebbled peak. Swallowing thickly, she met his gaze as his hand forayed lower until it rested, knuckles down, on the silk that covered the triangle of her dark, feminine curls.

"Think of this tonight, January."

Think? She could barely breathe. Through a hazy cloud of longing, she listened to his deep-voiced instructions.

"After I'm gone and you're lying here alone wondering what just happened, think of my hand loving your bare breast. Think of my mouth loving you there." He ground his knuckles gently against the sudden, liquid heat between her thighs. "And here. Think of me loving you here."

While she was still reeling from his blisteringly vivid mental images, he closed her robe, dropped a kiss on the top of her head, and walked swiftly to her bedroom door.

"I'll see you tomorrow," he promised, pausing to look back at her.

A protest—albeit a weak one—slipped out automatically. "But I have a full day's work I brought home from the office."

He grinned, undaunted. "So it'll be a study date. I've got an article to research. We'll work together. You'll never know I'm here."

Right, like a librarian wouldn't know she was surrounded by books, she thought, but she was grinning, too, as he gave her one last unflappable look, then left.

She wasn't grinning at five A.M. the next morning. And she hadn't wasted the long night on anything as mundane as sleep. Old and familiar dragons had reared their jeering heads and joined her in her virgin's bed. But the dragons spoke the truth, and she forced herself to listen.

What she'd gotten herself into with Michael Hayward was a major mess. She'd allowed him to get closer to her than she'd ever allowed any man, and she couldn't let him get to her again.

Even now, though, she toyed with the idea of trusting him with the truth of her past. Dangerous thoughts. Dangerous man. And she, a self-professed emotional cripple, had believed she could handle him by letting him take her to bed?

He'd caught her off guard, turning the tables by refusing her offer of sex. He'd talked of making love. He'd talked of commitment. She shivered and curled into a ball beneath her covers.

Face it, January, she told herself bluntly. *You're saddled with too many memories of a scarred childhood to ever be able to give of yourself in a relationship. Any relationship. Especially one with him. He's the last man you need in your life. Even if he weren't a threat to you professionally, you're not brave enough to set yourself up for the pain. And there will be pain,* she affirmed stoically. *When a man is involved, there is always pain.*

The wall was going back up immediately. When he stopped by that morning, she would send him away. Pig simple.

Not simple. Not even remotely simple, January realized when at eight A.M. she opened her door to a big bushy hound named George and Michael's good-morning smile.

Damn if she wasn't glad to see him.

He looked so good in his comfortable old jeans and sweater. He smelled of cinnamon and mint, and an added bonus. The zesty tang of the cool autumn morning clung to his jacket as he breezed through her door without so much as a "mind if I come in?"

"We brought rolls," he announced as he slipped past her, then plopped a smacking kiss on her cheek. "Coffee still hot?" he continued, disappearing into her kitchen.

After coaxing a surprisingly sedate George into the foyer, she closed the door. "So much for brick walls," she muttered under her breath. "And so much for firm resolve."

"They're getting cold," Michael called from the kitchen.

She had to end this now before she got used to seeing him show up at her door, she told herself. Before the gladness she felt when she saw his smile mushroomed into a longing to be part of the picture he'd painted last night. Before she lost the determination to send him away.

She followed the sound of his voice and, crossing her arms resolutely under her breasts, leaned against the kitchen doorframe. "Michael, this really isn't a good time for me. I told you, I have a lot to do today."

"It won't work," he said, giving her attempted brush-off about as much consideration as he might give a piece of lint. "I'm bigger than you are, so you can't make me leave. And I know you don't want to disappoint George. I promised him a day on your couch. Besides," he added, flashing her a boyish grin, "you don't really want me to go."

Helping himself to a mug of coffee, he settled into one of her kitchen chairs as if he cozied up to her table every morning.

"Michael, really—"

"I know what you're trying to do, you know, and I'm telling you it won't fly. You didn't sleep much last night, did you?" he asked around a mouthful of sweet roll. "Well neither did I. While you laid awake thinking up arguments against why we should give this thing a go, I was dreaming up rebuttals. I'm ready for you. So go ahead, fire one at me." He slouched back in the chair, looking smug and full of himself and playfully patronizing. "However, I feel it's only fair to warn you. I was captain of the debate team in college. Our last debate was on the positive aspects of toxic waste. We won. But don't let that bother you. Come on, give it your best shot."

He was incorrigible.

"What's the matter, Counselor? Haven't had enough time to prepare your brief?"

He was incredible.

"That isn't a smile sneaking up on you, is it?"

He was entirely too hard to resist.

Maybe just for today she'd let him stay.

"I like raisins," she said with feigned nonchalance, and joined him at the table. "Did you bring any with raisins?"

His grin was slow and sexy as he whipped out a huge frosted roll. Plump juicy raisins poked out of the folds of the pastry. "Do I know my woman or what?"

Her gaze danced to his, then away. *My woman.* She chose not to acknowledge that remark. Because if she did, she would have felt a warm all-over flush, a fuzzy, comfortable sense of belonging. She ignored it. And she didn't feel any of those things. Not one. Not one sweet, welcome yearning.

Michael intended to prove to his little doubting Thomasina that he didn't make promises he didn't plan to keep. He had promised her he wouldn't interfere with her work, so he didn't. After clearing the kitchen table, he deposited her on one corner of the couch. With George sleeping comfortably between them, he settled on the opposite end. They worked over their corresponding stacks of notes that way for the rest of the morning. He insisted only once that she take a break and join him and George on a quick trip around the block.

A little after one, with his rumbling stomach leading the attack, he foraged around in her frig until he found the makings for sandwiches. He made three. She nibbled on a half, deeply engrossed in the argument she was preparing.

Throughout the rest of the afternoon, he periodically scowled at her across the length of the sofa. She worked too hard. And she was damn near running on empty. The telltale signs were all there—the smudges of violet beneath her eyes, the slight droop in her shoulders, the delicate yawns she tried so hard to stifle.

By six-thirty, he'd seen enough.

"All right, Counselor," he said, standing before her. "It's time for all good little lawyers to call it a day."

She frowned up at him, her pencil poised over a thick yellow legal pad. "I'm almost finished," she said, and went back to work.

"You've got fifteen minutes," he warned her. "Fifteen minutes then you're done, whether you're finished or not. You're dead on your sweet little behind, January. It's time to knock off."

She mumbled something unintelligible and kept on writing.

He slipped out of the room and got busy in her kitchen. Fifteen minutes later, after drawing her a bath, he pulled the pencil from her hand and tapped the face of his watch.

"Time's up."

"Michael—"

"If you haven't got sense enough to take care of yourself, then I'll have to."

"I've been taking care of myself since I was sixteen," she snapped back, meeting his eyes with defiance.

She was past tired and more than a little bit cranky, he thought, and she didn't realize she'd just given him another piece of that precious pie.

"Then it's past time," he said, carefully removing her reading glasses and setting them aside, "that someone started looking after you."

Her eyes became as hard as onyx and he knew he was in for a battle. A bloody one.

"I don't need you or anyone else telling me what I can and cannot do, Hayward. I've put up with you today because you gave me no choice, but you've just crossed a line. I don't need your input. I don't need your opinions. And I sure as the world don't need you riding roughshod over my time. You know nothing about what I do and why I do it, so don't presume to know what's best for me."

Hunkering down in front of her, he folded her hands between his. Brushing his thumbs over her smooth, pale skin, he gazed at her, letting his concern show. "Then why don't you tell me? Tell me what drives you to work so hard, and maybe I'll understand.

"It can't be the money," he continued when she answered his request with silence. "You can't be getting rich on the kind of cases you handle. So if it's not the money, that leaves the motive. I guess I realized that the first time I heard you speak. And when I watched you in court, I saw your dedication again. But there's more, isn't there? You give until it hurts, January. Why?"

Her eyes suddenly looked a little wild, as if she felt she'd been boxed into a corner. Good, he thought. He wanted her to feel cornered. He wanted her to make that fatal mistake and tell him something about herself that she didn't want him to know.

"It's called involvement," she said finally, evasively.

"Involvement," he echoed. "Involvement to the point where everybody counts but you? Whatever happened to *you*, January? What happened that made what *you* want, what *you* need, take on such little value?"

He'd scored a direct hit on that one. He could see

it in her eyes, in the slight trembling of the hands he held. She tried to pull them away. He wouldn't let her.

"I run my own life, Hayward."

"Your work runs your life, Counselor, not you. You get involved in everybody's life but your own."

"My choice."

"Is it?"

Her eyes pleaded silently with him. "I'm trying to make a difference, Michael. Someone has to."

"My noble little lawyer," he said tenderly, "you *do* make a difference. I'm not disputing that. But there are a whole boatload of problems out there, and you're making a major-league mistake if you think you can fix them all."

"'No one makes a greater mistake than he who does nothing because he thinks he can only do a little,'" she quoted defensively. "Emanual Sawyer."

"To that, let me add, 'No one should try to solve the problems of the world to the exclusion of solving her own.' Michael Hayward."

"I don't have any problems," she insisted.

He squeezed her hands hard and decided she looked too tired for him to badger her any longer. "Yes, you do have a problem. You've got me, and my mother has always contended I'm the biggest problem the Good Lord in His infinite wisdom ever created."

She looked a little lost, a little frightened, and a lot relieved that he was letting her off the hook.

"Fair warning, January. Someday I'm going to know what makes you tick. Someday you're going to want to tell me. Until then, until you convince me you want me out of your life, I'm sticking tight. Come on, little heroine. Up." He rose and tugged her with him. "Like it or not, you're done working for today. It's time to save yourself."

He expected resistance, and he got it. But only a

little. Ignoring her grumbling protests, he led her to the bathroom where a hot, scented bath waited.

She eyed it suspiciously. "What's that?"

"Last time I looked, it was a bathtub," he said, his frown matching hers. "Now strip and soak while I finish fixing your dinner."

"Michael—"

"*January* . . . Much as I enjoy hearing you say my name, I'm getting a little tired of hearing it in just that tone. Could you try for a sultry purr next time?" He dropped a soft kiss on her forehead and shoved her gently into the bathroom. After letting her know her robe was hanging on the door, he closed it soundly behind him.

"Umm, Michael," she purred an hour later after she'd soaked and he'd fed her, then put her to bed, "this really isn't necessary."

He loved the sound of that purr. Soon he'd hear it for all the right reasons. Tonight he was willing to settle for the fact that he was making her feel better.

"It feels good, doesn't it?" he asked the back of her head as he continued massaging the tight muscles of her shoulders.

She sighed into the mattress and stretched all over. "It feels wonderful."

It was killing him. She was flower-scented and powder-soft from her bath, all warm flowing curves and bare satin skin beneath the heavy terry-cloth robe. And he was a mere mortal. A mere mortal who was about to burst out of his jeans.

"January?"

"Hmm?"

"I have to go."

She made a sound that vibrated with disappointment. He loved it! So, she didn't want him to leave. He was going to kiss her breathless as a reward.

"Turn over, love, and let me kiss you good-bye."

She tugged her robe around her as she shifted and twisted onto her back.

Slowly he bent his head to hers. "Let's make this a good one, okay? It's going to have to get me through the night."

It was better than good. It was better than bad. And it just kept getting worse. She met his mouth with open wonder and accepted his tongue with a silken promise, first yielding then boldly stroking until he wasn't certain she was going to get out of this with her innocence intact.

At last he pulled back and braced his fists on the bed, flanking her hips.

"I see you've been thinking about what I suggested last night."

She gave him a crooked little smile that made him think of sex and secrets and that black lace she'd almost spilled out of.

"You have a wicked smile, has anyone ever told you that?" he asked raggedly. "It makes me think about doing all kinds of things to you . . . things we'd both like but that are probably illegal in some states." He groaned at the openness of her expression. "And if you don't quit looking at me like that I'm going to have to teach you a lesson."

"A lesson?"

"Mm-hmm. Like what happens to little lawyers who ask for cases they're not ready to handle."

Suddenly they weren't playing anymore, Michael realized, and her eyes were doing her asking for her.

He had the answers to her questions. Every last one. And he wanted to give them to her so bad, it hurt.

"January," he whispered in defeat. Giving in to

an unforgiving need, he took her pretty, waiting mouth again.

When he'd sipped and suckled and wooed every ounce of longing from her lips, he trailed a string of slow, nibbling kisses from her jaw to her throat. He felt her tremble, and his heart swelled at the cause. It wasn't fear. It was desire. Undisguised, unrestrained, beautiful desire.

A bullet couldn't have stopped him then from nuzzling aside her robe and tasting the plump white flesh of her breast, the tight crest of her straining nipple.

She cried out and arched against him as he opened his mouth wide and drew her in with a gentle assault of teeth and tongue and suction.

Passion had never tasted so sweet. Like rich cream and melting honey, her firm flesh filled his mouth, consumed his senses, and beckoned him well past temptation into a dark, devastating swirl of desire.

"Michael . . ."

Her wanton whisper told him she was his for the taking.

Only he didn't want to take from this woman. He wanted to give. Tonight he was going to give until it hurt.

With a lingering, licking embrace of his mouth, he pulled away. He'd promised himself he'd wait until she was ready for this . . . ready emotionally as well as physically. One look in her eyes and he knew she wasn't ready for anything. She looked dazed, confused, and so incredibly sexy, he thought he'd go up in smoke.

He dropped a chaste good-bye kiss on the inner swell of her breast, then covered her with her robe.

"Will you be able to sleep now?" he asked, brushing a fall of dark hair away from her eyes.

She blinked that slow, sultry blink that turned

his insides to mush. He suppressed a groan, touched a hand to her flushed cheek, then rose stiffly.

"Good night, Counselor. Sweet dreams. I'll see you tomorrow."

"Michael . . ."

Her voice stopped him in the doorway. He turned slowly.

"Thank you . . . for today."

He tipped a finger to his forehead in a mock salute and flashed her a semblance of a grin. Then he hightailed it the hell out of there, before he crawled into her bed and buried himself so deep inside her that he'd never be willing to come out.

Six

As she got ready for work Monday morning, January was still thinking about the look on Michael's face when he'd left her. Of course, for the past two days she'd thought of little else but Michael. He was getting to her, getting to her bad, and she just couldn't let it continue.

All his talk about trust and commitment had made her lose focus. That focus, her whole life, had always been on her work. Michael made her want to turn her focus on him. On them. On what could happen between them if she let it. On the way he made her feel when he kissed her, the way he'd made love to her breast and then left her wanting so much more.

Well, there wasn't more, she told herself as she buttoned her blouse and slipped into her skirt. Nothing lasting, nothing permanent. Not with Michael. Even if he wasn't who he was, even if he didn't represent a threat to her work, she'd learned long ago not to trust anyone but herself. Commitment? Trust? They were only words. A good eraser or a little Liquid Paper and they were gone.

All you have to do is keep things in perspective,

she lectured herself as she ran a brush through her hair. *Call it your awakening from repression. Call it chemistry, but deal with it by calling a spade a spade, and under no circumstances by calling it love.*

Love, she'd learned as a child, was an empty emotion, a fallacy embraced by fools and dreamers. She was neither. As long as she remembered that, she'd be fine.

Grabbing her briefcase and coat, she left her house, thinking that now she had a handle on the situation, she would be able to hold her own.

It was a long drive from home to the office, though, and before she knew it, she was mentally fighting the war all over again, trying unsuccessfully to justify why she was wasting her time thinking about him.

He excited her, that was why. There wasn't any shame in admitting it, she told herself defensively. She'd like to meet the twenty-eight-year-old virgin who *didn't* get a little fluttery when a man as domineering as Michael Hayward tucked her into bed. In truth it was a relief to find out that her hormones hadn't really been dead all these years, but merely dormant. Her physical responses toward him were perfectly healthy, perfectly normal.

His advance and retreat tactics had baffled her for a bit, she admitted. Given a little distance from him, she now recognized that all his implied and stated concern for her well-being was a part of his ploy. Just another twist on the seduction plot. Like Saturday night when she'd served herself up on the proverbial silver platter and he'd put on the skids. Shoving aside the embarrassment that memory caused, she'd figured out that part too.

She was a novelty to him, a new experience for a man whose usual bed partners were no doubt as accomplished as he in the sexual arena. She represented the variety that put a little spice back into his life. As Helen theorized about her effect on Leonard, "I put the tick in his tock, sweetie. And I keep him so wound up, he doesn't know or care what time it is."

January suspected something similar had happened to Michael. Rather than intimidate or disgust him, her virginity gave him a new frontier to explore; and her secrecy about her past gave him another mystery to unravel.

"Enough, Stewart," she barked at herself. "You know how this story's going to end. Make up your mind to play it out and get it over with."

An affair was the answer, she knew. An adult, controlled, up-front unemotional affair that would expend all the sexual tension—and it *was* just sexual, she adamantly reminded herself—building between them. An affair made perfect sense, and they'd both be richer for the experience. As Michael had so clinically put it, she'd have her little biological embarrassment out of the way. For his part, he'd have the opportunity to live out his white-knight fantasy. When Michael ended it, as she was certain he would, she'd handle that too.

She felt a sinking pain at the thought, but by the time she pulled her car into the underground parking lot near her office building, it had dulled to a distant ache.

In the meantime she was pleased she had the issues pigeonholed and catalogued. And she'd step on her own foot if she ever found herself fighting this battle again.

Everything in January's life was back under control. At least it was until she opened the door to her office and found Michael perched on the corner of Helen's desk. Instantly, her meticulously woven arguments became about as cohesive as paper that had been run through a shredder.

"Good morning, Counselor."

His low, sexy greeting drizzled over her heart like warm honey. Not a good response. Not a good way to start her work day. She summoned up a scowl and issued a clipped "Good morning" as she breezed by him and on into her office.

There, she thought. She'd handled that with a minimum amount of effort. Then why were her hands shaking? And why did her heart feel like it had just been squeezed by a slow, kneading hand?

It wasn't because she was glad to see him. And it wasn't because he looked so sexy and sophisticated in his crisply knotted tie and tweed jacket, either, she argued, shrugging out of her coat and tossing it on the coatrack. It was because she was mad. Damn him, he had no right. No right to . . . to . . . to what, January? To look so mouth-wateringly gorgeous? To sit there in his civilized and proper clothes with that gypsy earring winking away, looking at her like he wanted to eat her alive, starting with her mouth and working down in slow, tantalizing nibbles?

She glared at him through the glass wall. The man was going to put her in a sanitarium. He was going to drive her flat-out, certifiably insane.

There he sat, laughing with Helen, no doubt sharing details on his weekend's conquest. They thought they were so cute, those two, all smug, knowing looks, all sweet secret smiles, just as cozy as two thieves splitting the loot.

Well, she had news for both of them. Inciting and inviting an affair was one thing. When it interfered with her work, it became something else, something she wouldn't tolerate. She'd tried to make that clear to him last night. She'd make damn sure he understood it this morning.

Marching back out of her office, she dropped the file folder containing her weekend's work on Helen's desk. "I'd estimate a good four hours of work ahead of you in there," she informed her starchily. "You might want to get to it. And Michael, I'd like to have a word with you, if you don't mind."

She'd seen hardened criminals quail when she used that tone of voice. Michael didn't have the decency to quail. Instead he grinned, a charming, disarming, rascal grin that almost—almost—weakened her resolve.

"Is she glad to see me or what?" he said in an aside to Helen as he unfolded himself from the desk.

"Muhammad should be so glad to see the mountain," Helen agreed with an exaggerated roll of her eyes. "Want me to hold your calls, sweetie?" she added, giving January a cheeky smile.

"That won't be necessary. This isn't going to take that long."

"Oooo," Helen cooed. "A quickie. I love it!"

Snapping Helen an I'll-deal-with-you-later scowl, January followed Michael into her office, then firmly closed the door behind her.

"Don't I get a proper good morning, Counselor?" His husky voice felt like the caress of his hand on her shoulder, like the brush of his mouth on her skin.

She suppressed a sensual shudder picturing what his definition of a proper good morning would entail. "Michael, we have to talk," she said, avoiding his eyes by concentrating on the thin silver stripe in his tie.

"Uh-uh. A proper good morning first." He took one prowling step toward her.

She straightened her shoulders, determined to lay her ground rules. "Michael, look," she said, trying to ignore the wild beating of her heart, "we need to get something straight right now."

"What we need to get straight," he said as he

cupped her shoulders in his broad hands, "is that you are having a morning-after attack of the jitters because of some of the things you're feeling about me right now. You're scared down to your pretty pink toes about how those kisses made you feel last night, and you're scared by the fact that you're beginning to want me in your life, and you don't know what to do about it.

"What we need to get straight"—he backed her up against the wall and nudged her with his hips—"is that you don't need to be afraid of what you're feeling. It's natural and beautiful and exactly the right reaction for a woman who cares about her man."

She read tenderness and passion and a wealth of unspoken longing in his eyes as he lowered his head. "What we need to get straight," he whispered, his warm breath mingling with hers, "is that I intend to stay in your life whether it scares you or not, because what I feel for you is as strong today as it was last night, and it's going to be just as strong tomorrow and every day after.

"What we need to get straight," he continued, unrelenting as he dropped a whispery kiss to each corner of her mouth, "is that it would be criminal to let one more moment go by before I do what we both want me to do."

Without another word he covered her mouth with his own, and taking his sweet, thorough time, he kissed her, romancing her into breathlessness with a slow and intimate embrace of hips and lips and tongue.

There was something . . . something she wanted to say, January thought distantly. For the life of her she couldn't remember what it was as with his gentleness alone he staked an uncontested claim to her remaining powers of reason.

All he had to do was touch her and she was too

busy feeling, too busy wanting, to remember what she'd so desperately needed to say. A new desperation had taken over, a desperation evoked by the sensual caress of his mouth and the delicious electric sensations shooting through her body everywhere he touched her.

Acting instead of reacting, she released her last fingerhold on sanity. Burying her hands in his hair, she lost her resolve to abandon.

Her response unleashed the waiting lion. No longer gentle, no longer sweet, his hands skimmed roughly down her sides, tunneling under her navy jacket to stroke her through the silk of her blouse. What liberties he didn't steal with his hands he plundered unmercifully with the crush of his body to hers, with the satin glide of his tongue inside her mouth.

They were both breathing hard when he finally pulled away. "And that, Counselor . . ." resting his forehead against hers, he paused for a recuperative breath. ". . . is what we need to get straight."

Leaning heavily against the wall for support, she blinked slowly and met the smoldering look in his eyes.

"Now that that's out of the way," he said, stroking his thumb across her lower lip, "let's talk about—"

He never finished his thought. The hazy, lazy moment was shattered by the riotous crack of breaking glass and Helen's sharp, shrill scream.

Before it registered that someone had thrown something through her window, Michael had flattened January against the wall again. Using his body as a shield, he protected her from the splintering glass that flew dangerously around the room.

The ear-splitting noise died abruptly. The momentary silence that followed was every bit as deafening.

"Are you all right?" Michael asked roughly, his blue eyes wild with concern as he stared down at her.

"I . . . I'm fine. Michael, what hap—"

He'd already pulled away. Rounding her desk at a run, he cleared the windowsill in one fluid stride and hit the pavement running. January got a glimpse of a small dark figure just before it disappeared at a breakneck pace around a corner. Michael, several steps behind, rounded the same corner at a dead run, his jacket flapping open at his sides.

Spotting a street brick in the corner of her office, she shivered, thinking about the murderous look in Michael's eyes. And she whispered a little prayer for the brick thrower.

"Good God almighty!" Helen, holding a hand over her heart, stepped gingerly into January's office. "I've never been so scared in my entire life! Honey, are you all right?"

When January nodded, Helen glanced from her to the gaping hole where the plate glass had been, then to the shards and splinters littering the room. "Why would someone do this?"

They were still wondering that when two hours later they'd neither seen nor heard from Michael.

The police had come and gone, taking both her statement and Helen's, then promising to look around the neighborhood for Michael. The building's maintenance man had managed to board up the hole until the window could be replaced the next day. January and Helen spent several more tense minutes cleaning up the mess.

By eleven o'clock January was past the point of worrying. Michael had been right. She did care about him, and she was frantic thinking about what could have happened to him.

Helen, ever the surrogate mother, decided to take January's mind off the episode. "I don't suppose you'd like to tell me how your date went Saturday night."

January shot an anxious glance toward the door. "No, I don't suppose I would," she said, then dumped a dustpanful of glass into the wastebasket. "You don't honestly expect me to believe Michael didn't tell you all about it."

"Michael isn't the kind of man who would kiss and tell," Helen said, sounding put out. "As far as I can see, it's his only flaw."

January grinned and took mercy. "We went to the Flagstaff House."

"And?"

"And it was nice."

"Nice," Helen repeated benignly. "He waltzes in here this morning, kisses you like he has intimate knowledge of your tonsils, and you expect me to believe your date was 'nice'? Come on, Jan. Who's kidding who? You don't earn a kiss like that after a 'nice' date. Well!" Helen returned January's glare with an affronted snort. "If you don't want witnesses, next time pull the blinds. Lord, that man can kiss!"

January sighed. "When they come to repair the window, get a bid on some dry wall, will you—something a certain secretary can't see through?"

Helen grinned sympathetically. "You're falling hard, aren't you, sweetie?"

She was saved from answering that distressingly accurate question by the door opening. A scraggly, surly-looking boy stepped into the office with Michael right behind him.

Aside from the fact that he looked haggard and disheveled, he appeared to be fine. She wasn't so sure about the boy. His size told her he could be anywhere from ten to fifteen years old. His eyes, however, said he was closer to fifty. She'd seen that kind of anger before. She'd also seen the despair. While she didn't recognize the child, she recognized the dark, threadbare jacket he was wearing and knew he was the one who'd thrown the brick.

She glanced from him to Michael. Both looked ready to chew nails.

"Helen," Michael said, "keep an eye on my friend here, would you? And you," he added to the boy in warning, "don't forget, we have a deal."

"I ain't your friend," the boy snarled, meeting Michael's gaze with defiance. "And I said I'd wait. So I'll wait."

"Fine. And don't give Helen any trouble."

The small slumped shoulders moved in what passed for an affirmative shrug, then he turned his scowl on Helen.

Decked out with a flashy new pink hairdo and a wildly painted blouse that she'd worn loose over black stretch pants and spike heels, Helen suddenly had a captive audience. The boy, it seemed, reacted to shock tactics. A geriatric punk rocker definitely represented a shock. As Michael ushered January into her office and closed the door behind them, the child was sitting spellbound while Helen offered him a cup of instant hot chocolate and pattered about some obscure rap group only a kid or a woman like Helen would know about.

Looking marginally the worse of the two, Michael slumped into the chair opposite January's desk and dragged his hands over his face.

"You okay?" she asked, easing a hip onto her desk.

He let out his breath with a weary puff and leaned forward, bracing his elbows on his widespread knees. Looking tired and troubled, he reached out and sandwiched her leg between his hands. With a slow caress, he ran his palms up and down the length of her calf. The touch wasn't sexual. She sensed instinctively that he simply needed to hold onto someone. Without questioning why, she was glad she was there for him. She also sensed that whatever was bothering him had less to do with the thrown brick than it did with the brick thrower. She could see it in his eyes. The child affected him. Deeply.

Intrigued, she asked again, "Michael, are you all right?"

He studied her leg for a long moment before he met her eyes. "Yeah. I'm fine. That little footrace just made me realize I'm getting to be an old man."

She smiled. "Hardly."

"Tell that to my body, toots. It's screaming bloody murder for the beating I just put it through. The little hellion runs like a damn deer. If he hadn't tripped over a garbage can in the alley, he'd be in Denver by now." He grinned crookedly, making a stab at masking his feelings, which she suspected were dark and brooding. His eyes betrayed the forced lightness in his tone.

She glanced through the glass wall to Helen and the boy, then back to Michael. "Are you going to tell me what happened?"

"Better yet, you're the expert. Why don't you tell me?" His voice was suddenly harsh, all pretense of levity gone. "Tell me what happens to make a kid hurl bricks through windows and talk like a gutter rat when he should be shooting baskets in his backyard and swiping cookies from his mom's cookie jar."

She remained silent, knowing he didn't really want an answer but an ear. He needed to talk. Even more, he needed her to listen.

He flipped off her pump, slumped back in the

chair, and flattened her foot on his thigh. His touch was intimate and familiar as he closed his hand over her stockinged foot and held on as if she were the link between right and wrong.

She tried to fight the softening taking place deep inside her. The children had always needed her. A man never had. Yet this man needed her now, and Lord help her, she wanted him to.

"His name is Toby Walters," he said with that same weary anger. "He's twelve years old, and he's never slept under the same roof for more than a year at a time since he was five. You know why he threw that brick through your window? He was aiming at my Bronco and missed." He laughed, but without humor. "Without laying it out in so many words, he told me he'd tried to break the Bronco's window for the sole reason that he resented the statement it made sitting by the curb. To Toby, it shouts success, independence, and power. All things that at some subconscious level he's come to realize he'll never have."

Michael's gaze was deeply troubled when he lifted it to hers. "How did he grow to the ripe old age of twelve and decide there isn't any hope?"

Damn her stupid heart, January thought. It was aching for him. "And you, Michael," she asked, forcing herself to meet the anguish in his eyes, "how did you grow to the ripe old age of thirty-eight and not know that the streets are full of kids like Toby?"

He looked away. "I know all about kids like Toby. I've just never *known* a Toby. How did I let that happen, January? How did I let myself become the kind of person who writes about life, but never actually gets involved in it?"

Fighting the urge to slip off the desk and fold him in her arms, she studied his dark head for a long moment. "He got to you good, didn't he?"

Michael rolled his eyes heavenward and shook his head. "When I caught up with him, I had to tackle him to slow him down. He fought like a marine. He was so small, and so damn scared . . . and so determined to be tough."

"And . . ."

"And I told him I wouldn't turn him in to juvenile hall if he'd talk to me." He snorted. "Toby told me to take a flying— Well, let's just say he told me what I could do with juvenile hall. So I bribed him with food. He was damned near starved to death."

January looked from Michael to the boy and understood what was happening here.

Toby's face was not a face you could easily love. To date, it appeared that no one had ever tried. At first glance his defiant, angry glare inspired fear, not affection. At second, it commanded a reluctant, distant sympathy that one so young could have become so hard. Yet as she watched him, all blustery indifference and foul mouth in the outer office, she took one long, searching look into his haunted, hollow eyes and melted. Michael had evidently done a little melting too.

"What now, Hayward?" she asked, watching him closely.

He shook his head. "I don't know. If we just let him go, the next time he decides to wreak a little havoc, someone might get hurt. What are his other options?"

This was the tricky part. She slipped her foot out of his hands, retrieved her pump, and settled behind her desk. "What does he want to do?"

"Who knows. The only reason he's even here is because I told him I'd pay him to tell me his life story." When she grinned, he shrugged. "Whatever works, right? The way he's got it figured, I'm just one more person using him. That's something he can relate to."

She studied his face for a long moment. "And what do you want to do, Michael?"

He didn't answer. He wasn't ready, she guessed, and decided to give him a little more time to think it through.

"Did he tell you where he lives?" she asked.

"With a cousin who has a bad habit of locking him out of the apartment when he leaves, which is often and for long stretches at a time."

She could see he was struggling between wanting to wash his hands of the whole dirty mess and trying to deal with a conscience that was telling him it was time to get involved.

"One phone call and I can have him off your hands," she said. "Human Services wouldn't hesitate to place him in an emergency foster home."

A muscle in his jaw worked hard before he tightened his lips and shook his head. Then he put voice to the private war she'd suspected he was waging. "I've had it so damn easy. All my life, I've had it easy. Peter Pan man, that's me. Fairy-tale childhood, fairy-tale career. I've got no worries, no problems." He scrubbed his face hard with his hands, then laughed grimly. "I can think of one time, one lousy time, that I've ever stopped to consider that what I was writing might affect someone's life other than mine, and that it might hurt them. It was a damn long time ago, and afterward I was so disgusted with myself, I decided I was never going to let something as sentimental as sympathy ever keep me from telling the whole story.

"But you know what happens to a man who makes decisions like that? *I'm* what happens. A man who views life and doesn't get involved in it is what happens. And you know what else? It's a hell of an awakening at this stage in my life to find out

I've still got a social conscience rattling around inside me."

Again he shook his head, as if accepting his decision but not knowing whether he liked what he was about to do. "I want to help that kid."

She listened, stunned, as he then told her what he wanted to do.

"Michael, this is crazy," she finally said. "Please think about what you're suggesting. I could expostulate for hours on the subject of abuse and neglect. I could quote you statistics that would make your mind rebel. I could give you odds—bad ones—on your chances of pulling this off. Even if we could get the court to agree, you have no idea what you're letting yourself in for."

"Then it's past time I find out, don't you think?"

She met his gaze levelly. "Why?"

"Maybe it's time someone other than you took on the task of saving the world."

She leaned back in her chair and studied him carefully. "If you're doing this to impress me, you're going to hurt that boy more than help him. If you're doing this to make yourself feel better about the fact that you had it good and he hasn't had anything but bad, you'll hurt him even more."

He looked, momentarily, like she'd slugged him in the solar plexus. "Low blow, January, but maybe I deserved it."

Rising, he strode across her office and stared distractedly at the degrees framed on her walls. "I can't even be insulted. I haven't ever given you reason to believe there are anything but self-serving bones in this body, have I? A man on the make, that's how you see me." He shrugged. "Maybe that's all I've ever shown you. Maybe that's all I've ever been. But you know something, Counselor?" He turned slowly to face her. "There is something about you that makes a man think past his own needs and makes him wonder about others. You rub off, January. You never do anything halfway. You commit completely. You make a man care. You make *this* man care."

The compassion and determination in his eyes touched a part of her heart that no man had ever touched before. With great effort she ignored that, ruthlessly focusing her attention on his proposition. He was a fool, she thought bleakly. But he was a sincere fool, and his mind was made up. The lawyer in her, however, offered one more chance at getting out. "You're absolutely sure you want to do this?"

He nodded.

She let out a deep breath. "Let me make a few calls."

Half an hour later, she had the necessary information on Toby. A couple more calls and she was his new court-appointed attorney. By the end of the hour, a messenger had delivered a copy of Toby's file, compiled over the years by the Department of Human Services.

It read like a bad movie. Deprived of even the most basic and elemental love by a mother who had deserted him as a toddler, robbed of a childhood by unethical foster parents intent on making money off the system, and finally neglected by the cousin who offered a home for the sole sake of a monthly welfare check he received on Toby's behalf, Toby had at last reached out for help.

"How does this happen?" Michael asked, his face a mirror of his anger.

January shrugged. "The system is overextended. Social workers are overworked, and they can't get an accurate read on everyone out there who's on the take. For every one hundred caring foster homes, there's the one bad one that slips through the cracks. Toby was unfortunate enough to be placed in a bad one, and then with his cousin."

According to the file, Toby was heading for big trouble. The brick wasn't his first cry against a system that had failed him. January had intimate knowledge of those cries. Trying to make sense of her father's abuse, then attempting to deal with his death alone,she'd cried out several times herself. Like Toby, she'd fallen in with a bad crowd and repeatedly gotten into scrapes with the law. Like him, her cries had gone unanswered until one overworked and underpaid social worker with a heart the size of Texas had looked past the anger and seen the pain. With her help January had turned her life around.

She watched Toby through the glass wall as he sprawled in feigned boredom in a chair. Toby didn't realize it yet, but Michael might just have the answer to his cry—*if* they could pull this off.

Twenty-four hours later Judge Lawton, his hawkish features set in a grim scowl, addressed January. "I don't have to remind you that what you've proposed is highly irregular. I am granting your requests and temporarily going along with your recommendations on the basis of your past performance and on your endorsement of Mr. Hayward and his family. In the meantime Human Services will be monitoring Toby's case closely and keeping me apprised of the situation."

They'd done it. They'd actually pulled it off. January breathed a sigh of relief. "Thank you, your honor."

He rapped the gavel sharply. "This court is adjourned."

With a last censuring glance at January and a swirl of his black robes,the judge exited the bench.

Behind her January heard the shuffling murmurs of the crowd milling out of the courtroom.

She remained seated, her hand, out of sight beneath the defendant's table, clasped firmly around Toby's. She wasn't even aware when she'd reached for him. His hand was shaking. So was hers. Not for the first time she hoped to heaven Michael knew what he was getting himself into.

Seeing that Michael had passed through the bar behind them and was approaching the table, she squeezed Toby's hand and offered a smile of encouragement. The boy looked up at her, his blue eyes cold, his small, childish mouth hard. Without breaking eye contact, he pulled his hand away, effectively erecting a barrier between them. He was a pro at building barriers, she thought. She and Toby were birds of a feather. She didn't try to recapture his hand.

"Do you understand what just happened, Toby?" she asked.

He glared at the glossy tabletop. "I ain't stupid."

"Why don't you explain it to me, January?" Michael intervened, easing a hip onto the edge of the table. "I'm a little fuzzy on the details."

Thanking Michael with her eyes for being sensitive to Toby's pride, she directed her explanation to Toby.

"Yesterday, after what happened at my office, I contacted Human Services and explained how your cousin has been neglecting you. Today the judge referred to a 'china' petition, remember? It's pronounced 'china' but it's spelled *C-I-N-A*, which stands for Child in Need of Assistance. The petition demands immediate action to get any child out of a bad living situation. So, according to the law, your cousin's neglect required the Department and the court to do something to help you right away. That's why we were granted a meeting with the judge today."

Though Toby's head was still down, she knew he was listening to every word. "Normally Human Services would appoint an attorney to represent your best interests," she continued, "but because the county attorney's office is overloaded right now, and because Michael and I requested it, the court agreed to let me represent you." She paused to give Toby time to absorb what she'd just told him.

"The judge agreed with our and the Department's contention that you needed to be removed from your cousin's home. Normally, the next thing to happen would be that you would be placed in an emergency foster home."

Toby squirmed in his chair. January was quick to reassure him. "I know you've had a bad experience in foster care, Toby, and neither Michael nor I wanted that to happen again. The judge agreed, and in light of the fact that there is a shortage of licensed foster homes with vacancies, has decided to place you in Michael's custody."

Toby glanced up at her. "I thought he said I couldn't stay with him."

She nodded. "You're right, the judge did say you couldn't stay with Michael, but he did award Michael temporary legal custody. Because Michael isn't married, the judge didn't feel he could provide you with a family home situation. That's where Michael's sister and her family come in. Just as soon as a foster care specialist conducts a study of their home this afternoon, you're going to be moving in with them."

January watched Toby's face carefully. She saw both understanding and resignation set in. Everything she'd said added up to temporary, not permanent.

But January knew something Toby didn't. January knew that Michael Hayward was one determined man. As of yesterday, she also knew Michael's sister, and that determination was a strong Hayward character trait. All of the Haywards would follow through with this commitment.

Late the previous afternoon, after they'd dutifully but reluctantly seen Toby settled into an emergency shelter as required by Human Services, Michael had taken her to meet his sister.

January had liked Gretchen Lockridge and her husband, David, on sight. Blue-eyed and dark-haired like her brother, Gretchen was a feminine counterpart to Michael, with the same quick smile and inquiring nature. Her husband, David, unlike the Haywards,hadn't had the cushion of financial security to pave his way. A self-made, successful businessman, he understood both poverty and despair. Though their backgrounds were vastly different, the mutual respect and love the Lockridges felt for each other had been evident as they'd listened to Michael. His explanation of Toby's situation had been met with compassion and then with enthusiasm for what Michael was proposing.

In the end Toby's fate had seemed predetermined. Gretchen, in the last two weeks of maternity leave after the birth of their second child, Andrea, had been agonizing over returning to her career in a Boulder advertising agency and leaving both Andrea and their four-year-old son Kevin with a child care provider. Toby and his obvious need put an end to her deliberation. Like her brother, she wanted to help. David supported her decision uncategorically, and by the time January and Michael had left the Lockridges' home that evening, they'd arrived at a plan of action. All they needed was a little luck and a favorable judge's ruling.

As January looked over Toby's head to Michael, they each breathed a sigh of relief that they'd gotten both.

"Come on, Toby," Michael said, placing a hand on the boy's shoulder. "There are some people I want you to meet."

Toby shrugged out from under Michael's hand.

"Toby," Michael said, hunkering down in front of the frightened boy, "I promise you things are going to be different from now on. I know it's been rough for you, and I want to change that. You're going to have to trust me on this one."

He glanced up at January, then went on. "Give me a chance to prove it's going to be different. What's happened to you in the past was unfortunate, and I can't explain why things didn't work out. There are wonderful foster families out there who want to help and who offer loving homes. You haven't been lucky enough to get hooked up with one . . . until now. And now your luck's about to change."

January watched as Toby struggled to keep a mask of bland indifference pulled over his emotions. Both she and Michael knew by now that Toby felt anything but indifferent. He was scared. He'd also eat dirt before he'd admit it.

At the ripe old age of twelve, Toby Walters was a cynic. Not a born cynic, but a carelessly nurtured one, learning from the school of hard knocks and a gross of broken promises that nothing in this world comes easy . . . and that talk is cheap.

Watching him, January suspected that was exactly what Toby was thinking now. He figured he'd just been paid a little more lip service to satisfy a system that had failed him at every turn. Just because one more judge had made one more ruling, it didn't mean his life was going to get any better. And just because someone said they cared, it didn't mean they did.

Seven

Michael, January was soon to discover, was determined to make Toby's life better. And in his bid to help Toby, he also gained ground on another goal to which he was equally committed: Winning her trust.

The wooing of January Stewart, as Helen delighted in referring to Michael's tactics, was sometimes subtle, sometimes sweeping, as every day in every way he showed her he was a factor to be reckoned with. He made it clear that he wasn't going away, not from her life and not from Toby's. At least not anytime soon.

Not that she wanted him to go, January admitted to herself one evening as she looked down at his dark head pillowed on her lap. She'd always been a loner by choice. Michael, however, by virtue of being Michael, had greatly depreciated the value she'd placed on solitude.

While he'd been relentless in his pursuit of what he teasingly promised would ultimately be her happiness, it was in the most conventional, most gentle of ways. He'd instinctively known that a series of elegant dinner dates and evenings at the theater weren't the approach to take with her. Instead he'd given her cherished glimpses of what it felt like to be young and foolish and falling in love.

He took both her and Toby roller-skating; on long playful romps with George; and to Toby's favorite spot, the carnival atmosphere of Pearl Street, where they listened to street-corner musicians and delighted in the antics of jugglers, sword swallowers, and stand-up comedians. He bought them silly and sentimental gifts, despite her many protests. And the night before, after pizza and after they'd dropped Toby off at Gretchen's, Michael, with a wicked glint in his eye and mischief on his mind, had taken her parking on Boulder's equivalent of lover's lane.

There, by the light of the radio dial and under the cover of soft music and heavily steamed-up windows, he'd pulled her onto his lap and informed her that he was about to enlighten her on the fine art of innocent necking and the thrill of clandestine petting.

He'd enlightened her out of her ever-loving mind. A man of great, giving passion, of fierce, breathless hunger, Michael had stirred the woman within her to a new and profound awareness. And he'd effortlessly fostered an appetite in her to match his own.

Shivering at the memory, she touched a hand to his hair and marveled that he'd taken her this far. A month ago she couldn't have handled a simple hug, much less this easy kind of intimacy. But as he'd promised, she had become used to him touching her. And as she'd feared, she had come to need his touch.

That day she'd had a grueling and disastrous session in court. Before Michael's intervention into her life, she would have wanted nothing more than to be left alone. Tonight, she needed him.

With Michael she felt alive. With Michael she indulged. And more and more often, with Michael she lived for today and forgot about the ghosts that haunted her. He made it so easy, sometimes, to forget.

This night, though, as much as she needed him, she couldn't forget. She felt tired and defeated, and the stigma of her past wouldn't leave her alone. Michael's part in it loomed like a shadowy prelude to pain.

Leaning her head back against the cushions, she closed her eyes, distantly aware of the low drone of the TV and the sweet scent of vanilla from the candle burning on the end table. One part of her wanted her past out in the open. Another was afraid. Afraid to trust in anything as superfluous as steamy midnight kisses and an emotion as fickle and as fallible as love.

"You're awfully quiet tonight."

She snapped her eyes open to see him frowning up at her, his gaze full of concern.

"You okay?" he asked.

She nodded and looked away, knowing her eyes told him she lied.

He didn't push, but she could tell he wanted to.

"Want some more popcorn?" he asked instead as he rose lazily to his feet.

She shook her head.

"Sure?"

"I'm sure."

She was sure of something else too, she thought as she watched him disappear into the kitchen to refill his bowl. The physical attraction between them grew stronger every day. She was dying a slow, lingering death waiting for him to take them to the end they both desperately wanted, but that he refused to give.

Her heavy sigh woke George, who promptly rose

to all fours. He stretched lazily and abandoned the rug in front of the TV for the spot Michael had vacated on the sofa. Absently stroking George's silky head, she realized she no longer approached lovemaking with Michael as a means to an end, or merely to satisfy her curiosity. She wanted to make love with Michael because he made her ache. He made her burn. He made her lose control when he touched her.

She felt her breasts tighten at the memory of last night's kisses. Her lower body clenched with the desire he'd been nurturing for weeks now. He'd taken her to the limit and beyond, and she didn't know how much more she could handle.

For the longest time she had tried to convince herself the attraction was purely physical, arguing that the sexual drive, after all, had been created for the express purpose of perpetuating the species. It was not designed to be easy to resist. Then, of course, there was Helen's perspective. "If the good Lord's only intent when He created men and women was to make babies, He'd never have invented black lace and water beds. Or whipped cream."

January had told herself repeatedly that it was chemistry, that there was nothing else between them.

She'd lied.

She missed Michael when he wasn't with her. She looked for him when she knew he was coming. And more and more often she found herself wishing she could truly become a part of his life.

Her heart tightened, then swelled as she watched him stride back into the room, watched the play of firm muscle beneath the denim of his jeans, the flex of sinew and bone, the black hair and flashing eyes that made him a beautiful, virile man.

A fresh bowl of popcorn in hand, he grinned

when he spotted George on the sofa. "Not that I blame you, old man, but that's my spot."

George pleaded dumb with a liquid look from his big black eyes, then snuggled his head deeper into January's lap.

"Up, George, now," Michael ordered sternly, "or you've seen your last milk bone, buddy."

George lay like a blanket.

Michael affected a scowl, then hit on the solution. "Where's the squirrel, George?"

Instantly alert, George bolted off the couch and trotted to the window to look, never realizing he'd been duped.

With a superior swagger, Michael settled quickly back into his place. Resting his head on January's lap again, he stretched his long legs out and sighed without an ounce of repentance.

Despite her melancholy mood, January grinned down at him. "That was sneaky."

"Hey, it's a dog-eat-dog world. He'd have done the same to me if he'd had the chance. Besides, the day I'm outmaneuvered by a mutt—no offense, George,—is the day I pack it in."

Discounting Helen, January had had little whimsy in her life. Consequently, it was this whimsical side of Michael she was drawn to most. His express interest in making her smile seemed so at odds with his status as an important and powerful journalist. His prowess was of a magnitude that made world leaders take notice. Whether he was chronicling the life of a film industry mogul, a Fortune 500 CEO, or a rebel leader in an underdeveloped South American country, no one wanted to be on the receiving end of a Michael Hayward exposé. He was tenacious to the point of employing seek-and-destroy tactics when he was hot on an assignment. He never left a stone unturned. Yet being with him like this, she found it increasingly hard to remember the man behind the reputation.

She had to be careful. He was a journalist first. That she was just a temporary diversion for him was the last thing she wanted to believe. Because she didn't want to believe it, it was the one thing she forced herself to remember, as well as that it was her mother's future as well as her own that was at stake if she confided in him.

"So." His voice drew her back to the moment. "What happened while I was gone?"

I accepted the fact that I'm in love with you, she thought bleakly, then shoved that knowledge aside until she had the strength to deal with it logically. "Three commercials and a station break," she said instead.

"Doesn't sound too exciting. In fact . . ." he set the popcorn on the floor and turned his attention to her, "the movie isn't too exciting. I wish you'd have let me take you out tonight."

She looked deep into the blue eyes that promised more than he could possibly deliver. "In or out, I wouldn't have been very good company."

"You had a rough day," he assessed accurately.

"Not as rough as my client."

"Can you tell me about it?"

Without breaking client confidentiality, she talked with him frequently about some of her cases. He seemed genuinely interested, and sharing with him provided a much needed outlet for her. Today's case, however, was different. This one hit very close to home.

The look on his face told her he sensed it. His insight scared the hell out of her. She countered the fear with weary anger. "Michael, why are you here?"

He studied her, frowning thoughtfully "Because you make the best popcorn in town?"

She looked away.

More softly he said, "Because you put up with my dog?"

When the smile he'd been playing for still didn't develop, he sat up and met her eye to eye. "Okay, what's this about, January?"

She hesitated, then drew a heavy breath. "It's about the fact that I don't understand why you're here . . . with me."

"Why *not* you?"

"Why not someone who can give back to a relationship as much as she takes?"

He was quiet for a long moment. "I ask you about your court case and you're suddenly talking about our relationship. What does one have to do with the other?"

Her heart jackhammered inside her breast. "Nothing," she lied. "One has nothing to do with the other. It's just . . . like you said. Today was rough."

"Tell me," he urged gently.

Focusing on a spot somewhere past his shoulder, she began, trying to keep any emotion from her voice. "My client was a desperate woman. She was fighting for sole custody of her three-year-old daughter. Today we tried to have the father's parental rights severed. Tried and failed."

"Why?"

His direct questions no longer intimidated her. She'd become used to them, and was grateful for the reminder that he was first and foremost a journalist.

"Why such drastic measures? He's a violent and abusive man, and my client felt the only hope for herself and her daughter was to force him completely out of their lives. Why did we lose? Because he is also a prominent and highly connected man from a wealthy and influential family. And because sometimes there is no justice in justice."

Feeling very tired, she pinched the bridge of her nose and closed her eyes.

Michael's hand dropped to her shoulder, resting there softly. "You can appeal."

She nodded once without enthusiasm. "And wait months for another court date. In the meantime, my client has to hear her daughter's cries when 'Daddy' comes to pick her up for visitation, then lie awake each night waiting for her baby's screams to ring through the darkness when the nightmares follow the visits."

She heard his deep intake of breath and knew he was fighting the same revulsion she was feeling.

"Is there no other recourse for them?"

"Nothing legal. If she refuses to let him see the little girl, she'll be held in contempt of court. In this case it would mean jail time, and then the father would have complete physical custody." She shuddered just thinking about it.

"What about supervised visits?"

"The judge wouldn't allow it. Said we hadn't clearly established that the child is in any danger, and it would be a violation of the father's rights." She tried to swallow back her anger. "Three psychologists testified, yet their professional opinions weren't, in the judge's words, conclusive."

His hand moved to the nape of her neck and kneaded consolingly. "What happens now? She can't just quit fighting."

The compassion in his voice was almost her undoing. "She hasn't."

His eyes narrowed as comprehension dawned. "She's going underground, isn't she?"

Her silence confirmed his suspicion.

"January, you could face disbarment if you have a hand in arranging that."

Without conscious thought, she cupped his cheek in her hand. His concern touched her deeply. No one but Helen had ever been concerned about her before. "Your worry is misplaced. I didn't arrange it. I'm not even certain it's going to happen. If I receive a call from Judge Lawton telling me my client is in contempt of court for not delivering the little girl for her scheduled visit tomorrow, I'll know that she decided to go under."

She became quiet, thoughtful. "Frankly, I don't know what I'd do if she had asked me for that kind of help. While I don't have connections, I'm well aware of the Underground Railroad. The network it rumored to be strong and supportive. If I were faced with a decision to help, I'd hate to think I'd refuse, and in doing so be a passive party to the horror that little girl has to endure if her father remains a part of her life."

"But is a life of constant running and hiding, of leaving behind family and friends such a healthy alternative?"

"The key word is alternative," she said firmly, and while she had the courage she added, "at least she'd have an alternative. She deserves that much. Every child does."

The room became deadly still, like the calm in the eye of a storm, or the pregnant silence before the last piece of shattered glass falls from a broken window. Beside her she could feel Michael's body grow bowstring tight.

"And you, January," he asked quietly, "were you ever offered an alternative?"

Her eyes snapped to his. "I—I don't know what you're talking about."

He gazed at her solemnly. "Who made you so afraid to trust, January?"

Her heart tripped into double time. She looked away as her body began a deep, uncontrollable trembling. *Do it!* some reckless inner voice cried. *Tell him! Test him.*

"January . . ." His voice was a gentle assurance in the pulsing silence.

One glance at the tortured look in his eyes sent her near to the edge. She was tired of believing he would betray her, that he represented a danger to her future because of her past. But years of conditioning wouldn't allow her to trust him with the entire truth.

No force on earth, however, could hold back the questions that had always haunted her.

"Why couldn't my mother have done that, Michael? Why couldn't she have fought for us? Why couldn't she have fought for me? Why did she let him hurt her? Hurt . . . me?" Her voice broke on the last word and she bit her lip to keep from crumbling.

She was so tired. She'd been strong for too long, needy for too long. She needed now. She needed to know she was a person of value, that someone thought she was worth fighting for, worth taking, even if it meant taking a chance.

"Michael, hold me."

With a groan born from her anguish, Michael pulled her into his arms. He held her fiercely, rocking her, soothing her with his hands in her hair, pressing her cheek against his shoulder.

Her heartbreaking questions confirmed what he'd long suspected. And they explained so much—her initial resistance to physical contact, the undercurrent of distrust, the fact that she'd never before let any man close to her. It hadn't been just a man that had abused her. It had been her father, the man who should have been protecting her.

It explained so much, but not nearly enough. Not enough to help him heal all the hurts she carried inside her. Not enough to dispel all his dark, horrible thoughts of what she may have gone through.

His work had led him into danger more than

once, had placed him in life or death situations where it could have come down to killing or being killed. He'd been prepared to face that if he had to, no matter how loathsome the thought of taking a man's life was. But here, on this sofa with this strong yet fragile woman in his arms, he feared he'd kill and kill gladly if he ever got his hands on the man who'd done this to her. Or the woman who had stood by and let it happen.

Along with his anger, he felt a consuming sense of helplessness. There were words—he was sure there were words he should say to let her know she no longer had to handle this alone. He was a man of words, made his living with words. Yet holding her against him, feeling her strength dissolve into despair, he couldn't string two coherent, let alone consoling, words together.

But the simple fact was, she didn't want words from him tonight. The bold, sensual pressure of her body against his told him what she wanted. She wanted strength. And she wanted action.

No warning, however distant, no argument, however valid, could stop him from tipping her face up to his. He didn't pause to question if it was the right thing to do. She was reaching out as she never had before, and he reacted instinctively to the need in her voice, to the desperate yearning of her body.

She moved against him with a restless urgency as he captured her mouth in a soulful, searing kiss. He catered to the hunger with which she returned his kiss and to the gut-tightening clutch of desire arrowing through his groin. And he clung by a thumbnail to the knowledge that for her sake he'd have to take it slow.

Slow because a distant unattainable fantasy, though, when she writhed in his arms like a sudden summer storm. She was all wild, untamed energy, all crackling electric heat. Her ardor was a mind-numbing, loin-thickening reality as she met his open-mouth kisses with hot, liquid passion.

"January," he gasped, coming up for air. "Baby . . . sweetheart . . . easy."

She didn't want easy. She groped for the hem of his sweater, and when she found it, dragged it roughly up and over his head. While he was still recovering from her aggression, she peeled off her own sweater, then unhooked and shrugged out of her bra.

"Michael, I need you . . . need you," she whispered urgently as she rose to her knees beside him and guided his mouth to her breast.

He lost it then, all reason, all control. The taste of that plump breast filling his mouth, the feel of her tight, straining nipple against his marauding tongue, shattered any hope of taking her gently. By offering herself so wantonly, she was doing the taking. He was helpless to do anything but follow her lead. She drugged him with her throaty murmurs, drove him wild with her sexy shivers.

With a groan of utter defeat, he sank with her to the carpet, then scrambled as frantically as she to rid himself of the rest of his clothes.

When she was naked and writhing beneath him, he parted her thighs, found her wet, swollen core, and thought he'd die before he became one with that tight, silken heat.

A moment of sanity gripped him. "January." He breathed her name like a prayer against her mouth. "I don't want to hurt you."

She rocked her hips against him in an instinctive and innocently provocative gesture of submission. "Michael, please . . . don't stop now. Don't do that to me!"

The desperation in her voice tore at him as a

flood of desire swamped him. Yet he tried, Lord, he tried.

"Sweetheart," he gasped between harsh breaths, "I have to know . . . are you protected?"

Her eyes flew open. "No. No!" she whispered, looking like she might cry. "Aren't you . . . don't you . . . have something?"

Had he not been so needy and she so proud, he might have laughed at the exasperation in her voice and at her crestfallen expression. "I didn't exactly plan this, love." He pressed his lips against her breast and asked hoarsely, "When was your last period?"

He felt her body stiffen with embarrassment.

Cupping her face in his hands, he stroked away the tension with a steady caress of his thumbs over her temples. "Think, baby. When?"

Her nipples grazed his chest with each shivery breath she took. He groaned and repeated on an urgent growl, "When?"

"Two . . . three days ago."

Reacting to the sudden uncertainty in her voice, he brushed a kiss across her brow. "It's okay. It should be a safe time for you."

The dim light from the TV and the soft flicker of the burning candle revealed another question hovering in her dark eyes, one he felt compelled to answer. "And you're safe with me. I would never put you at risk, January. You don't have to be afraid I'd leave you with anything you don't want."

She wilted momentarily, then met his gaze with barely banked longing. "Then love me."

Whispering her name, he covered her mouth with his and eased into her.

She was incredibly hot, impossibly tight. The exquisite clench of her body around him stole his last vestige of control and drove him to the ultimate barrier. On a long, deep stroke, he reached resistance. She stiffened and cried his name.

For too long he'd teased them both with simmering kisses and slow, sensual caresses; too many times he'd brought them to the brink of this act, then withdrawn. There'd be no turning back tonight.

Swallowing her cry, he plunged deep, experiencing a moment of blinding self-hatred as he felt her virginal shield resist, then tear. She gasped and struggled against him even as he languished in the wonderful way she gloved and pulsed around him.

Achingly aware that his pleasure caused her discomfort, but helpless to make himself leave her, he praised her with whispered endearments, scattering soft, pleading kisses over her face.

"Don't fight . . . please baby . . . try to relax, and the pain will ease."

He stroked damp hair from her brow and watched as she swallowed huge breaths, forcing herself to do as he instructed.

"Better?" he asked, as he sensed the tension leave her.

She nodded and licked her kiss-swollen lips.

He chased her tongue back inside her mouth and bit it lightly before losing himself again in a long, breathless kiss. On a groan of passion too long denied, he began moving inside her.

Slow and shallow, he stroked her, then faster and deeper as her body conformed to the size of him, and she rose against him in pleasure instead of pain. But the reality of loving her was more powerful than the expectation had ever been, and too soon he lost the ability to pace, to hold back for her sake.

Her body gripped him like a tight velvet fist, sweetly milking him of his strength, greedily stripping him of his control. On a riotous rush of sheer animal need, he cried out her name and plunged deep, spilling his passion, losing himself in the rich, mind-melting haven she offered.

Inside her austere suburban house all things remained the same. In the background the TV droned softly and the flickering candle threw dancing shadows across the ceiling. George whined in his sleep and curled into a tighter ball on the rug by the window.

But January Stewart was irrevocably changed.

At twenty-eight, the loss of her virginity should have been cause for celebration. That a man like Michael—a man she loved—had taken it should have been cause for joy. Yet the room's unnatural quiet where moments ago there had been thunder invited neither.

Something was drastically wrong. She could feel it in the controlled way Michael's breath fanned her shoulder, in the undeniable thread of tension strung through the powerful male body pressed against her side. Yes, something was wrong . . . and she knew without questioning why that it was her fault.

She shivered involuntarily. Michael reached across her and snagged the quilt from the sofa. Without a word he covered them both, then lay on his back beside her. Stacking his hands beneath his head, he stared broodingly at the ceiling.

She wanted to dissolve like a stain into the carpet. Since that wasn't an option, and since she could no longer stand his censuring silence, she sat up, clutched the quilt to her breast, and reached for her discarded sweater.

A gentle hand on her arm stayed her.

Statue-still, she closed her eyes and waited.

"I'm sorry, January." His soft words grated like fingernails scraping across a blackboard. His silence had already told her how sorry he was. It hurt more somehow to actually hear the words. Had it been good for him, he wouldn't feel the need to apologize. Had she known how to please him, she wouldn't feel so foolish.

She bowed her head and huddled deeper inside herself. "It's all right," she said, feeling awkward and inadequate and anything but all right.

He swore fiercely and in one smooth motion tugged her back down onto her back. Looming over her he met her eyes with a look of unbridled anger. "There is nothing right about it." He sucked in a deep breath and closed his eyes. When he opened them again, they were dark with his effort to stay under control. "Are you all right? Did I hurt you?"

"I'm fine," she answered pridefully.

"Dammit, you are not fine. And I'm the biggest fool to ever unzip a fly."

She rolled her head to the side, avoiding his look of disgust.

"I promised you we'd make love," he went on angrily, "and instead I practically attack you! Your first time and I got so wrapped up in wanting you I took you on the floor. On the *floor*, for God's sake!"

She turned to face him, shaken by the self-loathing in his voice. In his eyes she saw something that made her stop and rethink everything he had said. Vulnerability. The censure in his voice had been unmistakable, but the one he was blaming was himself. He wasn't disappointed in her for being inadequate, but in himself for losing control.

If relief were sweeter, she'd have died from it. If love were stronger, she couldn't have borne it.

Touching a hand to his hair, she met his eyes with a direct and forgiving gaze. "If there was an attack, Michael, I'm the one who launched it."

He shook his head. "I was rough with you. I didn't want it to be like that. . . . But lady, you took me by storm, and before I knew what was happening, it was all over but the thunder." He pressed her hand, palm open, against his chest where she could feel his heart still rumbling like the distant reminder of that storm. "I wanted to go so slow with you."

With a sharp feminine thrill, she felt him growing hard once more where his hips pressed against her thigh.

"And dammit, here I am . . . already wanting you again."

Emboldened and inflamed by his arousal, she moved against him and offered a solution. "Then go slow. This time . . . go slow."

He smiled and gave her a blood-thickening, pulse-quickening kiss, then picked her up and carried her to her bed. Taking a washcloth from the bathroom and ignoring her embarrassed protests, he gently and thoroughly washed both the proof of his passion and the proof of her innocence from her thighs.

Then, as though time didn't exist or ceased to matter, he proceeded to teach her a whole new definition of slow.

Slow became the smooth glide of his fingers across her face. Slow became the unforgivingly lanquid journey of his mouth as it charted an erotic, seductive course across her heated skin.

She moaned and sank deeper into the covers, not at all sure she was going to survive slow, as with timeless, torturous leisure he introduced her to sensations she'd never dreamed existed, to pleasures so exquisite they flirted with pain, and finally to a love she'd never believed was real.

She rose to meet his hot lazy kisses, arched into his lush tongue strokes as he made love to her breast, reshaping her with his clever hands, suckling her with a stunning combination of lips and teeth and tongue.

With the same sensuous fervor, he worshiped the pale flesh of her belly before moving on to the sensitive silk of her inner thighs, where he incited her to a restless, reckless yearning for more of what was yet unknown.

Breathless, she cried his name.

Shameless, she begged him for more until, when she was drugged from his passionate loving yet feeling more alive than she'd ever felt a right to be, he finally poised above her.

Stunned, exalted, she opened to him like a long-shaded window to the first sweet promise of sunshine.

His mouth covered the moan that escaped her parted lips as he entered her . . . slow . . . full . . . throbbing.

And the sensations began again. Deeper this time, richer, as he filled a void she had never known was so empty, completed a story she'd never known had such a glorious end.

With his tenderness and honest passion he penetrated a barrier that was as emotional as it was physical and opened a pathway for trust to break through.

Eight

Michael recovered slowly. January was wrapped tightly in his arms, the heat from her body lulling him, her sweet scent surrounding him. She lay so still, it was a long while before he realized she was awake and staring into the darkness.

He nuzzled the underside of her jaw, discovering a spot he hadn't yet explored to his satisfaction.

"I take it the lady liked slow," he whispered.

She groaned and burrowed deeper under the covers.

The hand lazily caressing her breast stilled. "What's this?" he asked, coming up on one elbow.

She shook her head.

He leaned across her and switched on the bedside light.

"Uh-uh," he murmured, tugging down the sheet she'd drawn over her face. He watched, fascinated, as a slow, pretty blush crept up her neck and flooded her cheeks. Finally, *finally,* he understood.

So it took a ton of bricks to penetrate his thick skull. He was entitled to a little post-ecstasy stupidity . . . but not at her expense. She'd left him breathless. Evidently she'd left him senseless, too, or he'd have recognized her insecurity right away.

"Don't hide from me, January." He touched her face. He couldn't stop touching her. "Not ever. I want to see how you look after I love you. I want to see that beautiful flush on your cheeks and know I put it there."

He pushed the sheet lower, then watched in reverent fascination as he framed a lush white breast in the V between his thumb and index finger. "I want to see your pretty breasts, all rosy and swollen from my mouth. And here," he whispered, sliding the sheet even lower. Very gently he traced the curve of her waist, the sharp, delicate point of her hip, then the smooth skin of her inner thigh. "I want to see you here."

As a kid and at his sexual peak he'd never been a marathon man. Yet this woman, with just a look, repeatedly turned him to steel. Enthralled, he watched the slender lines of her throat as she swallowed and met his eyes, eyes he knew had gone all languid and smoky again with newly fired passion. For her sake he banked it.

"Lord, you are beautiful," he murmured. "Do you have any idea what it does to a man when a woman comes apart for him the way you did for me? The way you moved beneath me, the low, lusty sounds you made?"

She shook her head.

He smiled because he realized she honestly didn't know. "It makes him think he owns the whole circus, sweetheart." He leaned down and whispered a kiss over her pink nipple, then suckled it into a tight velvet peak. "It makes him want to leap tall buildings, beat on his chest with his fists, and shout to the world at large that he's a man. A man with a woman who satisfies him like no other woman ever has."

That finally won him a smile . . . a smile laced with tentative and surprised pride and so much vulnerability, it made his heart ache. With a possessive groan he drew her against his side. "And makes him think he can slay his lady's dragons," he added, tucking her head under his chin.

Immediately she stiffened, sensing the direction his conversation was leading.

"No, baby, don't," he said, knowing he was rushing her but needing this from her now more than ever. "Talk to me, January." He pulled back so he could see her face. "Tell me what he did to hurt you, so I can make it better."

She tried to look away. He wouldn't let her.

"After what we just shared," he said, "you've got to know how much I care about you. Don't shut me out any longer."

"It's too much, Michael," she said, shaking her head. "And too soon. I need a little time to get used to . . ." She made a vague gesture to the room in general. ". . . to all of this."

"Time," he echoed, unable to conceal the hurt in his voice. "Time to figure out more ways to hide you feelings like you just tried to hide your body?"

When she bit her bottom lip and held her silence, he swore softly. "January, I have tried," he said, as disappointment and anger knotted in his gut. "Dammit, I've tried to give you time. Now I need something from you. What just happened between us was spectacular, and I won't believe for a minute that you weren't responding to me emotionally as well as physically. Your reactions were honest and real and the intensity rocked me to my toenails. But don't you see that if you still can't trust me, then we made love for all the wrong reasons?"

He clawed a hand through his hair, struggling to find a way to make her understand his frustration.

"As wonderful as it was, I let you down tonight," he said, his voice gentling. "I swore that when we made love, it would be after you realized you could trust me."

"I do trust you," she insisted.

"With your body," he said, feeling defeated.

Her eyes were pleading and overbright as she touched a hand to his cheek. "Yes."

He turned his mouth into her palm. "It's not enough."

Tears crowded her eyes, and when she spoke it was in a soft, tortured whisper. "It's as much as I'm capable of. It's more than I ever thought possible. Please, Michael, can't you accept it as enough?"

"You still don't get it, do you?" He heard the ache in his voice and didn't try to conceal it. "You still don't realize that I love you."

Her beautiful brown eyes darkened with what he refused to accept was fear.

"Don't do this," she begged.

"I'm not doing anything. You're the one who's reducing this to conditions." Frustrated, he lay back and stared sightlessly at the ceiling.

He couldn't believe what was happening. They'd just shared something that should have ended with a sense of beauty and bonding. He'd told her what he'd never told another woman, and she was acting like he'd committed murder.

She cared for him. Dammit, she loved him, he knew she did! What he didn't know was why she wouldn't let herself accept it.

Sighing heavily he turned his head on the pillow. She was watching him. The look in her eyes finally made him realize that if there was one truth in what she was telling him, it was that she needed more time.

Think, man, he mentally blasted himself. If he'd learned anything from dealing with Toby, it was that a child who'd been the victim of abuse or neglect repressed the feelings that hurt him the most. It was his only way to deal with the pain and still survive. January wasn't a child. That didn't mean her memories weren't still painful. If what Toby's psychologist told him ran true to form, then January, too, had been dealing—or not dealing—with her memories for years by shoving them as far away as she could. Tonight she'd given him a glimpse of the past that haunted her. He'd be a fool to think she'd be ready yet to entrust him with traumas she'd spent a lifetime suppressing.

He'd be a bigger fool if he didn't give her the time she asked for. She was worth the wait. If the way she had come alive in his arms that night was any indication of what lay in store, she was worth *any* wait.

Groaning, he again pulled her against his side, "Okay," he whispered, pressing his lips to her temple. "I'll accept your conditions—for now. But someday, January, you are going to realize you can count on me. For anything. For everything. Nothing you've done, nothing that's happened to you, could make me love you less. Nothing."

The tension was slow to leave her, yet he could feel her relax muscle by muscle until she finally snuggled sleepily against him. He consoled himself with this little show of trust. *One piece at a time, Hayward,* he told himself. *Take it as she gives it, one piece at a time.*

He held her long after she drifted into a deep, exhausted sleep, long after his arm had lost circulation, long after the ache of disappointment had ebbed. For the first time in his life he wanted something he couldn't have. For the first time in his life he was going to bite the bullet and wait for it.

• • •

Thanksgiving morning dawned cool and sunny, a gorgeous epilogue to the first measurable snowfall of the season—six solid inches of white over Boulder and the surrounding area.

It was a gloriously beautiful day, and January, wrapped up for so long in the day-to-day demands of her work, had forgotten the magic and the allure of the mountains.

The ride in Michael's Bronco to the Hayward cabin was like a drive through a Courier and Ives painting. It was pristine, beautiful, and breathtakingly quiet . . . except for an occasional deep "woof" from George when he felt he wasn't getting his share of their attention.

The only way she could have enjoyed the drive more was if she felt comfortable with the fact that she'd let Michael talk her into joining his family's celebration.

There was little he couldn't talk her into these days. She stole a glance at his classic profile as he maneuvered the Bronco around the snow-covered mountain curves. Since that night two weeks ago when they'd first made love, she seemed incapable of denying him anything . . . anything but the one thing he wanted: Her total trust and commitment.

Though he hadn't pressed her again, she knew he was quietly waiting. She could see it in his eyes, in the openness with which he shared himself with her, in the passionate desperation with which he sometimes made love to her.

What happened between them physically was so powerful. She hadn't counted on that. Nor had she been prepared for the strength of the emotions she'd been so determined to keep at a distance. Michael was just as determined to close that distance. Of the two, he was infinitely more successful.

As a lover he was more sensitive than she'd ever imagined a man could be. He gave her pleasure selflessly and in ways she'd never dreamed possible. He was tender and gentle. Demanding and exciting. Innovative and shocking. And insatiable.

He overwhelmed her; he thrilled her. And since that first night, he'd refused to let her hide behind uncertainty or self-doubt. With a masterful, insightful awareness, he'd freed her of her inhibitions. By giving and taking with equal measure, and by laying bare his own vulnerabilities, he'd shown her how to conquer her own.

Feeling a flush of arousal creep up on her, January dragged her thoughts away from a vivid memory of his lovemaking and looked out the Bronco's window. As the Christmas-card scenery shuttled by, she wondered at the direction their relationship was taking. Ironically it was the bond of their past that linked them together while ultimately keeping them apart.

Michael was still not aware of that bond; awareness was with her always. Awareness of a secret she'd locked away and of the pain that would be reincarnated if it came out in the open.

It was a time she didn't want to remember. It was a time she could never forget. Michael would always represent a reminder.

Though it had been difficult for her to let go of her initial anger, she'd long since realized the man she knew now was a far cry from the self-serving opportunist he'd appeared to be back then. And she no longer believed he would use the past against her. In truth she wasn't sure she had ever believed it. That particular argument had been a convenient and safe shield to hide behind while she was being bombarded with all the emotional bombs involvement with him had precipitated.

The problem now was how to make herself tell him the truth about her past. The remaining barriers—shame and fear and years of denial and secrecy—were as massive as the Rockies. And always, carved like a commandment in her psyche, was the reality of rejection. Would he still want her, could he possibly still love her, after he found out where she'd come from, what she'd done?

"We're here," he announced, snapping her back to the world around her.

She murmured a disbelieving "Oh" as he negotiated the final curve and, gunning the motor, coaxed the Bronco through a snow drift and over the final crest.

The cabin offered a welcome diversion from her suddenly dismal thoughts. She fell in love with it on sight.

Woodsmoke curled from a massive stone chimney that took up nearly the entire west end of the huge two-story log structure. The sills of the many multipaned windows were heavily laden with snow, as were the wraparound deck and the wood-shingled roof, from its sloping eaves to its towering peak.

"Oh, Michael. It's perfect."

"It ought to be." He grinned as he killed the engine and set the parking brake. "Every weekend since I can remember we spent hours up here making sure it was built to Dad's specifications."

"You built it?"

"Actually Dad did, but Rob and I provided a little muscle and a lot of sass before it was all said and done."

His pride in both his family and their mountain retreat was evident as, with George bounding ahead of them through the snow, he guided her toward the door.

The splendor didn't end on the outside. What the Hayward men had accomplished in structural design, the women had complemented with their decorating of the open, airy interior.

Homespun had never looked so good, from the multicolored braided rugs scattered across the polished tongue-and-groove floors, to the handmade quilts hanging on the natural wood-paneled walls and draped over heavy handcrafted furniture. Antique copper pieces and intricately woven baskets of every size and color and shape hung from open beams, nestled on the stone hearth of the central fireplace, huddled in every conceivable nook and cranny, and were filled with pungent eucalyptus. Everywhere were framed and matted pictures of the Hayward family at work, at play, at rest.

The cabin shouted welcome, as did the aromas wafting from the kitchen area and the smiles that greeted her and Michael as they shrugged out of the coats.

Michael's mother, Norma, vigorously wiping her hands on a dish towel, and his father, James, tucking a newspaper under his arm, came forward to welcome them.

After giving her oldest son a fierce hug, Norma turned to January. "We are delighted you agreed to join us today," she said graciously.

"Roughly translated," James put in, extending a hand to January and a quick wink to Michael, "she means it's about time the prodigal here brought you around to meet us."

Norma swatted James with her dish towel. "Don't pay attention to him, January. To a man, the Haywards are notorious louts."

Laughing at the affronted snorts Michael and his father manufactured, January turned to find a younger version of Michael waiting for her with a huge so-you're-the-one grin on his face.

Blue eyes much like the ones January now knew Michael had inherited from his mother danced with mischief as Rob turned a blast of charm on her.

"Give me half an hour alone with her, big brother," Rob said, his smile never dimming and his gaze never leaving January's face. "It's time someone clues the lady in."

"You'll have to forgive him, January." Michael draped a possessive arm around her shoulders. "Rob's the baby of the family. Twenty-nine years old and he hasn't yet figured out that if he wants to live to see thirty, he's got to have my permission." To Rob, he added serenely, "Does the expression 'over my dead body' mean anything to you?"

"You would think," Norma said fussily as she guided January out of the thick of the good-natured squabbling, "that grown men would have the good sense to not show their immaturity in front of God and everybody. When you two decide you can behave," she added over her shoulder, "you can have her back. That is, if she wants to join you. Heaven only knows why that would be."

Waving hellos to Gretchen, who was changing the baby on a huge, overstuffed sofa, and to David, who, with Kevin on his lap, was trying to coax James back to the cribbage game in progress, January followed Norma to the kitchen end of the great room. Toby, without any urging, offered both January and Michael a quick "hi" while he unselfconsciously lavished his affection on George. The dog was alternately licking his face and trying to knock him down with his exuberant canine version of hello.

And there ended January's reservations about being an outsider joining what was so traditionally a family gathering. To a person, the Haywards were warm and charming and made her feel like it was the most natural thing in the world for her to be a part of the clan. And their equally easy acceptance of Toby was heartwarming.

Thanksgiving dinner was more than just a special family meal for the Haywards. It was an event. Toby, his cheeks bright red from a recent romp in the snow with Michael and George, put it best as he took in the huge trestle table laden with a banquet-size feast.

"Wow!" he exclaimed, forgetting he was a tough guy who wasn't supposed to act excited or be impressed. "I saw something like this once in a magazine, but I didn't know real people actually ever had this much food."

It was a stunning commentary on all he'd never had. The healthy glow in his eyes, however, and the fact that more and more often the child hidden behind the facade of a man broke through, were testimony to how well things were going.

Gretchen and David were doing a wonderful job with Toby. The weekly court-ordered counseling sessions he attended were also having a positive effect, and were helping him express his anger constructively. And wonder of wonders, he openly displayed genuine affection and protective instincts toward little Andrea, along with a thinly veiled pride at playing big brother to Kevin.

January, though, had realized from the beginning that it was Michael he came alive for, Michael who truly brought out the child inside Toby and heightened his capacity for trust.

As the entire family gathered around the table, she looked over Toby's head to Michael and caught him watching her with that patient, knowing look that never failed to make her heart clutch and then soften.

How she loved him, she thought, indulging in the admission she rarely let herself make. She loved him and she was going to lose him if she couldn't make herself trust him with the truth of her past. And there was the rub. If she didn't tell him soon, she would lose. Yet once he found out, she'd most likely lose anyway. She tore her gaze away, unable to bear thinking about what would happen then.

Avoiding his eyes and thoughts of the inevitable for the remainder of the meal, she forced herself to join in on the lighthearted table banter.

After helping wash the dinner dishes she settled into a window seat overlooking a gentle slope of aspens and pines, where the Hayward men and boys had begun the expansive task of building a snow fort.

An expected contentment crept over her. Instead of fighting the feeling, she gave in to it. If only for today, she wanted to experience this rich sense of family. Tomorrow was soon enough to face the aching reality that she'd never really had one, not in the Hayward sense of the word.

"I don't believe I've ever seen Michael so . . ." Norma's soft voice drew January's attention from the window. Michael's mother had quietly joined her and was watching the snow construction. ". . . carefree," she finally decided. "Toby's good for him."

"They're good for each other," January said, smiling as Michael, in a sneak attack, pelted Toby with a snowball. He collapsed with dramatic flare when Toby retaliated with a direct hit to the middle of Michael's chest. Her smile widened when Toby jumped on Michael and the two of them wrestled and rolled in the snow until Rob complained that they were goldbricking.

"I was beginning to wonder," Norma went on, "if that oldest son of mine was ever going to tire of his restless ways and settle down."

"Toby is very important to him," January said carefully, sensing Norma's conversation might be heading in another direction. "Michael takes his commitment to him seriously."

"Toby isn't the only reason Michael has changed."

Uncomfortable with Norma's comment, January purposefully kept her gaze on the action outside. "Michael is his own man," she began hesitantly. "I'm not sure anyone could influence him if he didn't want to be."

"Exactly," Norma agreed, grinning.

They watched in silence for a while as the building gave way to a full-fledged, no-holds-barred snowball fight.

"I'd always hoped," Norma said after a minute, "that when he finally decided on a woman, he would make a good choice. He had me worried for the longest time, but not anymore." She laid a gentle hand on January's shoulder. "He didn't let me down."

Evidently the look in January's eyes tickled her, because she laughed. "Surely you realize that he's in love with you. Oh, dear. I can see you're having a little trouble with that. Well, don't worry. I have every confidence he'll convince you."

January was saved from making a stammering fool of herself when Michael burst through the door with a blast of cold air and bellowed, "January! They're whaling the tar out of us. We need reinforcements fast!"

Grateful for the interruption, she scrambled into her boots and coat and laughingly joined the fray.

"This," January purred several hours later when, wrapped in nothing but the fire's glow and Michael, she stroked a renegade lock of hair back from his forehead, "is absolutely decadent."

"I promised you decadent," he whispered, nudging her chin with his nose so he could nibble on her throat. "I just had to get rid of a few Haywards before I could deliver."

She smiled and arched her neck, giving him better access. "I loved your family. I was sorry to see them leave."

"Oh, were you now? That's not the impression I got when you threw me to the floor and started ripping my clothes off an hour ago."

She laughed and tugged playfully on his hair. "Conceited jerk. I did *not* throw you to the floor. I may have pushed a little—"

"A lot. You pushed a lot. You couldn't wait to get me on this bear rug."

Her voice went all low and husky. "I couldn't wait to get you *bare* on this rug."

"Lord, I love a woman who knows what she wants."

And he loved January most just this way, Michael added to himself. Get her out of those stuffy suits and her lawyer mode, and there wasn't a woman alive who had more fire, or more softness. The only thing he liked to see her in more than a pair of jeans and a sweat shirt was nothing at all. And he had her the way he wanted her now, naked and spent in the afterglow of their lovemaking.

Watching her with his family had been like watching several kids in the proverbial candy store. They'd loved her. And he believed her easy admission that she felt the same. She hadn't even thought before she'd said it. It had just slipped out, unqualified, uncontested, like so many things she said to him these days.

Since the first night they'd made love, it just kept getting sweeter. He'd been right not to push her. Her feelings for him were evolving naturally, and if he wasn't mistaken, she was close to accepting the fact that she loved him . . . without conditions.

He'd felt a little guilty about letting Toby return to Boulder with Gretchen and David. But Kevin had insisted that both Toby and George come home with them. Toby had beamed at being so much in demand, and in the end Michael had relented. Besides, he had hopes that spending the rest of the holiday weekend alone with January could prove to be the turning point in their relationship. Solitude for two had its advantages, and he intended to take every advantage as it presented itself. Starting with right now.

"This has always been one of my fantasies," he confessed, sliding slowly down her body, tasting and exploring and enticing as he went. "Making love to you here with nothing but the mountains and the firelight to distract you."

"*One* of your fantasies?"

"Mm-hmm." He circled her nipple lazily with his tongue. "One of many. With you—lord, you're sweet—I find my imagination is boundless. For instance," he murmured, working his way back to her mouth with studied leisure, "it drives me crazy thinking about loving you with your glasses on."

She moved sinuously beneath him and ran her palms down the length of his back. "You'd look pretty silly wearing my glasses."

He smiled against her mouth. "And you've got a major attitude for a woman who's about to be ravished."

"Ravished?" She grinned, considering that. "I could live with ravished."

In a heartbeat she took him from a mere whisper of smoke to a fire that fed on her flame. He pulled away from her, his sudden need transforming their love-play to serious intent. Drawing her with him until they were on their knees facing each other before the fire, he kissed her long and deep.

"You are so beautiful." He ran his hands down her back, reveling in her long sleek lines, the satiny smoothness of her skin. Cupping her bottom in his palms, he urged her close, then sank down to his haunches and pressed his mouth to her belly. He loved her texture, her heat, the way her muscles quivered and tightened against his tongue.

"You taste wonderful," he told her. "So sweet. So wild."

Her fingers tunneled through his hair. She arched her back, restless for more, pressing herself against his mouth.

"You like that?" Whispering heated love-words, he covered her breasts with his hands, aware that his breath was escaping in harsh, heavy gusts. "Tell me what else you like, love. Tell me. It's yours. Anything. Everything. Just tell me."

She told him.

He groaned at the urgency in her throaty voice, at the need in her breathless plea. Lowering her quickly to her back, he cradled her hips in his hands and gazed at her up the length of her body.

"Open your eyes, January. I want to see them when I love you."

She did as he asked, and he saw her eyes were glazed with desire. Only then did he touch her lightly with his mouth. She cried his name and reached for him. He touched her deeper. She tangled her hands in his hair and on a long, shuddering moan came apart for him.

He lost himself in the honeyed taste of her, in the wild, uninhibited way she writhed in response to his erotically intimate, profoundly beautiful expression of love. Her abandon inflamed him, and his love for her blinded him to anything but the way she entrusted herself without reservation to his keeping.

Driven by her cries, he stroked her past the point of pleasure and into a realm of deep, consuming passion. She was weeping softly when he finally rose above her.

With the firelight casting dancing shadows across their bodies, he buried himself inside her. Embracing both the body she offered and the accompanying sense of absolute communion, he committed to her completely.

It ceased to matter at which point she began and he ended. The only thing that mattered was that she was his woman, the embodiment of his wildest dreams, and that he loved her with everything that made him a man.

His release came on a deep, powerful thrust, a climax as ultimate as it was irrevocable, as beautiful as the sound of his name on her lips as she found her own fulfillment, her body clenching and tightening around him.

Long, silken moments later, he rolled onto his back, taking her with him. Exhausted, deliriously sated, he lay spread-eagle on the fur rug with her sprawled across his chest.

"It's never been like this for me," he whispered, a little awed at his gruff admission.

"It's always been like this for me," she murmured, brushing her fingers across his chest. "Since the first time you touched me. Since the first time you told me you wanted to make love with me." She raised her head so she could see his face. Her gaze, though heavy-lidded in the aftermath of passion, was fierce and sure. "I love you, Michael. I didn't want to . . . I'm still not sure I should, but I do. With everything that is me, with everything that I have, I love you."

He'd waited a lifetime to find her, had endured a

private, painful hell waiting for her to say those words. Hearing them now, seeing the proof in her eyes, he felt a fullness he could compare to nothing he'd ever experienced.

He closed his eyes against the pressure building behind them. "You are the damnedest woman," he said raggedly. "And you picked the damnedest time to spring an admission like that on a man. I'm out of commission, Counselor. I can't do a thing to show you how much I needed to hear you say that."

Locking her gaze with his, she eased slowly down the length of his body. "It's not up to you to show me anything," she whispered huskily. "It's my turn to show you."

"January . . ." He sucked in a harsh breath and dropped a hand to her tangled hair. "Baby, sweetheart, I can't . . ."

She touched him, tentatively, inexpertly, but with so much love he groaned and burned and bucked against the shimmering caress of her mouth.

Her eyes were dark and liquid, her smile sultry and victorious with the knowledge that she'd proved him wrong.

Loving her more than life, he knotted his hands in her hair. Helpless to stop her, he succumbed to her slow, velvet torture and to the blissful, consuming oblivion of her selfless loving.

Nine

It was late the next morning when January slipped out of Michael's bed. Shivering as the cold air hit her naked skin, she found a navy blue robe—probably Michael's—and wrapped it around her.

Downstairs, she stared out the kitchen window, deciding that beyond a doubt, this was the most beautiful morning of her life. Even with the brilliance of daylight clarifying what she'd done, she didn't regret confessing her love to him.

Set free, her love grew in layers, drifting softly around her like the snow that was accumulating again outside. A distant dread niggled at her, for experience, her best and most formidable teacher, had taught her that anything this good wouldn't be allowed to last. But she wasn't going to let herself think about that. Not today, not when life seemed as full as a goose-down quilt and as perfect as the man sleeping under one in the big bed at the top of the stairs.

Grinning proudly at the first fire she'd ever coaxed to life in a fireplace, she dug around in the cupboards until she found a skillet.

The eggs were done and she'd just finished

setting the table when Michael, looking sinfully rumpled and beautifully mussed in nothing but bare feet and blue jeans, sauntered down the stairs and into the kitchen.

Would her heart never fail to melt at the sight of him? she wondered, stepping into his arms and returning his warm, lazy kiss.

She nestled against him as he looped his wrists at the small of her back. "We're looking very domestic this morning," he murmured in a voice as sleepy as his smile. His gaze strayed to the table before returning to prowl her face and her own sleep-tousled hair. "And very sexy."

She brushed the hair from his eyes, then reluctantly disengaged herself from his arms. "You'd better be hungry."

His patented bad-boy grin suggested he was.

"For eggs, Hayward." Arching a chastising brow, she returned to the stove. "I hope you like them scrambled. Now sit. Eat."

"Domestic, sexy, and bossy," he said, sounding intrigued. Making it obvious he was enjoying himself immensely, he sat back and watched her fuss around, serving him his breakfast. "And subservient. Interesting. This has definite possibilities, Counselor. We might be able to negotiate a deal here. How does me, lord and master, you, cook and love slave, strike you?"

"And last night you accused *me* of having a problem with attitude." With a cheeky grin she sat down across from him and reached for a piece of toast.

He caught her hand. Laughing, she met his gaze across the table.

"Okay," he said, sobering abruptly. "How does me, loving husband, you, adored wife, sound instead?"

She stared transfixed, as all traces of teasing

vanished from his face. His eyes, too, had darkened. They searched hers with a probing, heated intensity.

Her smile froze. The crackle of the fire, a soft whisper of wind scuttling around the corner of the cabin, and the plaintive beat of her rapidly hammering heart were the only sounds in the suddenly quiet room.

She'd sensed this was coming. In all honesty she'd even wanted—just once—to hear the words. She'd wanted the proof that she'd been wrong, that she meant something more to him than a diversionary affair.

Tears stung her eyes, reminding her of all the things she wanted. If they were to have a future, she'd have to tell him the truth. Faced with that reality, she realized she could never tell him, that she'd only been fooling herself into believing she could. She was too much of a coward.

The panic she felt at the thought of him finding out about her past was so profound, it paralyzed her with fear. If he learned about the travesty that was her childhood, about the lie that was her life, he'd never be able to look at her again with anything but pity and disgust. And after experiencing his love, her pride would never allow it.

Aware of his eyes quietly assessing her, she pulled herself together and laughed nervously. "Would you listen to him," she implored the ceiling. "He doesn't know what he's saying. One day in the wilderness and the man already has cabin fever."

She knew he saw right through her pitiful attempt to avoid dealing with his proposal. But even with her trembling voice betraying her, she kept it up, praying he wouldn't corner her, that he wouldn't press his advantage.

"Eat your breakfast, Michael," she said, trying

for playful but achieving only pathetic. "Food will give you strength of mind and body. Heaven knows, you must need it. Then we'll get you outside and clear the cobwebs from that poor addled little brain of yours. You'll be thinking straight again in no time."

Never more aware of the inevitability of losing him, she forced herself to hold his gaze. She wanted today so badly. She wanted tomorrow. Several tomorrows. But she wouldn't even have the rest of the weekend if he insisted on pushing this now.

Blessedly, if belatedly, he released her hand and slouched back in his chair. "You step one foot outside that door," he warned, "and you're doomed."

"Doomed?" she asked on a thready whisper. She knew she'd hurt him. His eyes revealed a raw and unmistakable pain.

He nodded gravely. "I saw you in action yesterday, Stewart. Now it hurts me to have to be the one to tell you this, but you can't throw a snowball for love or money."

He was giving her an out, she realized. The pressure in her chest eased. The ache behind her eyes, however, intensified. She watched his face carefully as he drizzled honey over his toast, and with feigned arrogance added, "Of course, If you *do* offer me money, I might decide to go easy on you."

Grasping at the straw he was offering, she forced herself to play along. "Go easy on me? You forget, Hayward," she said with false brightness, "I saw *your* form yesterday too. You throw like an old lady."

He cocked a dark brow. "An old lady?"

Ignoring the dangerous glint in his eyes, she reached across the table for the honey so she'd have something to do with her hands. "You'll be begging for mercy before the end of my first volley."

He snagged her wrist and with little effort pulled her around the table and onto his lap.

"Mercy, she says."

A wicked grin crawled up one side of his mouth. Though his manner was playful, his eyes were still hard and hurting. "We'll see who begs for mercy. As a matter of fact . . ." He cleared away his breakfast dishes with a negligent sweep of his hand. ". . . I'm open to the idea of entertaining a little begging right now."

Gripping her by the waist, he lifted her and set her in front of him on the edge of the table. His eyes narrowed dangerously as he moved his chair closer and, taking his slow, deliberate time about it, untied and opened her robe.

Locking his gaze on hers, he slid his hands in an agonizingly slow journey up the length of her thighs. She shivered with a mixture of apprehension and desire as he forced her legs apart and slipped between them.

"Michael . . ." she gasped.

"That's a good start, Counselor," he said. Then he reached for the honey dipper. "Let's see if you can do better."

January watched the play of muscles over Michael's back as he fed the evening fire. When he settled back down on the sofa, she snuggled against his side like a docile, sleepy puppy.

She was exhausted, but pleasantly so. Michael had wanted her exhausted, and that morning he'd told her as much. He wanted her defenseless, her guard down, the way she'd been when he'd made love to her on the table.

His proper little Victorian lawyer, as he was so fond of calling her, had turned into a wild, uninhibited wanton. She suppressed a groan, recalling how she'd been willing to tell him anything, to promise him anything . . . anything but what he thought he wanted to hear.

Marriage. The word brought a cold, clammy sweat to her palms and a wild, desperate terror to her heart.

He touched her hair. "Did my little snow bunny hop a little too hard today?"

She smiled despite her troubled thoughts. "It's only because I'm saving my strength to breathe that I'm letting you get by with that condescending, sexist remark."

"You mean you're not my little snow bunny?"

That earned him a semi-aggressive elbow in the ribs.

He grunted, then laughed. "You're just sore because I clobbered you good in the snowball war."

"I'm sore," she countered gravely, "because you had me traipsing up and down thirty acres of timber like a mountain goat."

"You saw some beautiful scenery, didn't you?"

"Breathtaking. I'm going to hate leaving here Sunday. You must have such wonderful memories of spending your weekends and vacations here with your family."

She heard loneliness creep into her voice, the longing for something she'd never had. She hoped he hadn't heard it too.

He had, of course. He heard everything.

"You don't ever have to leave if you don't want to," he said. "It's yours, January. Yours for the taking. I tried to offer it to you this morning, but you didn't want to listen."

He wasn't any better at concealing his hurt than she was, she thought. She had hurt him badly that morning. The pain poured out with every word.

"Talk to me," he commanded softly.

She didn't have to ask what he wanted to talk about. She didn't have to see his face to know he was tired of waiting. She could feel the tension in his body, the frustration in his hands as he held her.

The frustration wasn't all his. She couldn't bear the thought of losing him. It had haunted her all day as she'd tried to come to terms with the fact that she would lose him. If she trusted him with the truth of her past, she'd lose him. If she didn't tell him, she'd still lose.

Wanting to hold onto him for as long as she could, she'd concluded, out of desperation, to compromise. He needed something from her. She'd give it, but only enough to satisfy his curiosity. Not enough to condemn her.

But since revealing any part of her past was going to be difficult, she hedged. "How easy?"

"How easy, what?"

She heard the impatience in his voice and knew he was struggling to control it.

"You told me once that you'd always had it easy. Now that I've met your family, I understand where you get your confidence. How easy was it for you to sustain it? I mean, are we talking captain of the football team here, or water boy?"

He gave her a hard look. "For the record I want you to know that I realize what you're doing. You're stalling . . . and very badly, I might add."

She sighed deeply.

"I know it's hard, babe, so I'm going to play it your way, okay? Just don't push me too far. It's show-and-tell time, Counselor. Before this night is over, I expect you to spill it. All of it. Are we clear?"

She nodded grimly.

He gentled his edict with a caressing kiss to her forehead. "Good. But please keep in mind that it's going to take everything in me not to throttle you into cutting the damn small talk. Now, what was the question?"

She cleared her throat delicately. "Captain or water boy?"

He snorted. "I'll have you know you're lying in the arms of one of U.S.C.'s finest tight ends ever to catch a forward pass."

She smiled against his chest, loving him, knowing he was trying to make it easy for her. "I wouldn't touch that line with a hot pad."

"I've always been big on contact sports."

She chuckled. "I think I'll let that one go by too."

"Chicken." He gave her a quick hug. "Speaking of chickens—and pay attention here, because this is a brilliant segue designed to loosen your tongue—when did your transformation to legal eagle begin?"

She groaned. "That wasn't brilliant. It was awful. I think we need to get you out of the high altitude."

"Nothing on earth could compel me to leave this sofa or back away from this conversation. It's already been too long coming. Now answer the question."

"Actually," she admitted after a deep breath, "transformation is a good word. Just substitute jailbird for chicken." She squeezed her eyes shut while the impact of her remark settled. Telling him even that hurt more than she'd anticipated. Her heart slammed erratically against her chest. Instinctively she tried to put some distance between them. He only tightened his arms around her.

"There is nothing," he said firmly, "that you can tell me that is going to make a difference in how I feel about you. Nothing. I love you, January."

She knotted her fingers around a fistful of his sweater. "This is so hard."

"I know, love. But what's more difficult, now? Telling or concealing? January, it's past time for secrets between us."

Secrets. She felt her body tighten into one huge, aching knot. Her life was based on secrets. And lies. Would her half-truths help or complicate the issue?

"Come on, babe. I started with something you should feel comfortable with. Tell me why you chose law."

"Law. You're right. That should be an easy one." Focusing on the blue-orange glow of the flickering fire, she drew a steadying breath. "I finally realized I wanted control of my life and that I could have it if I knew how to deal with the system." She hesitated. "Like Toby, I knew all about the system."

"How are you like Toby?"

She sifted and sorted and finally decided to be direct. "Because I was angry, and for similar reasons. Toby doesn't know his parents, and that hurts him. I knew mine. And that hurt me."

"Tell me."

She closed her eyes, feeling both fear and anger. And a profound sense of foreboding. Michael's heartbeat was steady and strong beneath her cheek, and it gave her courage.

"My father was a drinker. My mother was . . . she was very weak. She couldn't help it. She was a classic enabler. She let him abuse her. And when he got tired of beating on her, he turned to me. Not an original scenario, nothing unique."

"Except that it happened to you," he said, his voice gruff, his arms again tightening around her.

"Except that it happened to me," she agreed softly. "When I was thirteen . . ." She paused, flashing on a picture of her father lying dead, a pool of blood staining the floor beside her bed. Her heart leaped uncontrollably.

"What happened, love?" Michael asked gently.

She brushed a damning tear from her eye. "My father . . . died." Her coward's heart convinced her that what Michael didn't know couldn't hurt him and what she let him know wouldn't hurt her . . . at least not as much as the whole truth.

"I went a little wild after that," she rushed on, knowing that if she didn't elaborate, Michael would assume her father had drunk himself to death. "Mother had a lot of difficulty dealing with . . . many things. She couldn't cope with her own problems and wouldn't deal with mine. Short and to the point, I got into some trouble. A little recreational trouble, a little shoplifting trouble." She shivered, and he held her tight as she told him the minor and not so minor laws she'd broken. "I dropped out of school and ended up in and out of a number of juvenile detention centers."

"You must have been a terror," he whispered against her hair.

His attempt at humor didn't fool her for a second. She'd stunned him. Shocked him, even. And his mood was anything but light.

"I thought I was real tough, all right. What I was, however, was stupid. I was eighteen before I woke up and realized I was just another unfortunate statistic—a high school dropout with a record, no money, and no future. It made me even angrier. I didn't want to be just another anything."

"And then," he prodded gently.

"And then, with the help of a wonderful woman who saw past the anger, I decided that if my life was going to change, I was the one who was going to have to do something about it."

"Just like that."

She shrugged. "I got my GED while I was still in detention, applied for some educational grants and loans, and earned an associate's degree at a small community college. I managed to get my GPA high enough to be accepted here at Colorado State on several financial-needs-based scholarships. The rest, as they say, is history."

"Wrong." He tipped her face up to his. "The rest, like the best, is yet to be." He kissed her, pouring into that kiss a world of hunger, a world of hurt. Hurt he felt for her. Hurt, she knew, he thought he could heal. She clung tightly to that notion, wishing it were so. When she was in his arms, when he was loving her, anything seemed possible.

"Marry me," he said fiercely, then frowned as panic flashed in her eyes. "It wasn't supposed to sound like a threat. Baby, you had to know this was coming."

"It can't happen."

"You love me," he insisted.

"I love you," she said without hesitation. "Can't we be satisfied with that?"

"Satisfied? Satisfied implies pleased, gratified. You're saying let's settle. I will not 'settle' for anything when it comes to you. I don't want an affair, January. I want the whole package, wrapped in pretty paper and a big satin bow. Love, marriage, Toby . . . our own babies."

"Michael—"

"No." Sensing her arguments, he cut her off. "Don't do this, January. And don't sit there and try to convince yourself you know what's best for me, because you don't know. But I *do* know what's best for you. Me."

"You are the best thing that's ever happened in my life," she admitted sadly.

"Then what is it?" He searched her eyes. "Is there more? More you're afraid to tell me?"

She looked away. Hating herself for lying, she shook her head.

"Then you're missing something here." Gripping her shoulders gently, he made her face him. "You just told me honestly about all those deep, dreaded secrets you thought were going to send me packing. Haven't you noticed? I'm still here. I'm not even looking toward the door."

But you will, she thought, fighting a pain that could only be heartache. *If you ever find out what a coward I am, you will.* She met his eyes and felt the cold bath of guilt wash over her.

"January, listen to me. I've never experienced anything like what happens when we come together. Obsession has taken on new meaning since you've entered my life. Possession is a word I fight daily because I know you wouldn't stand for it. Believe me when I tell you, I'd never try to run your life. I want to marry you. Have babies with you. And if you want, I'll even try to save the world with you."

A tear fell, uninvited. "No marriage, Michael. No babies."

He closed his eyes and swallowed a vicious curse. "Tell me why."

She couldn't answer him.

"Tell me, January, or you'll force me to tell you."

She bolted out of his arms and off the sofa.

He was silent for a long moment. It wasn't until he spoke that she realized he'd walked up close behind her. "You are not a defenseless child any longer. Your father can't hurt you anymore."

Forcibly repressing a shudder, she wrapped her arms around her waist and stared vacantly out the window into the night. "He will always hurt me."

"Only if you let him. You didn't deserve all the things he did to you. And you are entitled to all the things he didn't do for you." He ran a gentle hand down her arm. "Don't you think I realize why you're fighting this? Why you won't let yourself take what someone should have given you long ago?

"I've seen you with Toby. I've seen the way you look at him, the way you want to reach out and wrap yourself around him. And then I see you draw back. You're afraid to let yourself commit to him, just like you're afraid to commit to me. You're afraid that at some point we'll both reject you."

She couldn't look at him. Couldn't let him see how close he was getting to her most secret fears.

"Those are a child's fears, January," he said as if reading her mind. "A child who had reason to fear. But you're a woman now. And you are loved. No one treasured you as a child. Let me treasure you now."

She whirled around to face him. "Don't you see?" she cried, overcome with guilt and love and a fierce need to protect him. "It's because I love you that I can't marry you. Michael . . . the odds of a child growing up in a home as dysfunctional as mine was and evolving into an adult who can perform successfully in the role of spouse and parent are somewhere between slim and none."

"Perform?" He practically spat the word. "Dysfunctional? I'm not asking for a statistical report here, Counselor. I'm asking for a woman, with a woman's needs, a woman's strengths . . . and a woman's weaknesses. You are that woman. You are *the* woman. The only one I've ever asked to be my wife. The only one who has ever made me feel complete."

"Sometimes," she whispered, throwing herself into his arms and burying her face against his throat, "sometimes you almost convince me it could work."

"Oh, it'll work, January." He held her tightly against his chest. "Haven't you heard? I never make a mistake, not professionally, not personally. It's against the law."

"In my experience, it's Murphy's Law that takes precedence over all others," she said dismally. "Anything that can go wrong, will."

"Then maybe," he countered, cradling her head in his big hands and tipping her face up to his, "it's time we set some new precedents. Tell me you love me," he demanded, his eyes growing dark.

"I love you."

"Tell me you'll at least think about this."

Because at that moment she couldn't deny him, because she couldn't help herself, she nodded. "I'll think about it."

For the next several days January did nothing but think about it. Helen made sure of it.

"Why do you think you have to be everybody's heroine but your own?" Helen asked one morning after several days of uncharacteristically silent speculation.

January glanced across her desk at Helen, who had interrupted her dictation to pose the question.

"That's ridiculous."

"The only thing ridiculous about it is that it's true. I may be old, sweetie, but I'm not blind. Things between you and Michael should be as sweet as powdered sugar on a strawberry margarita. Yet you're as sour as a kosher dill. You think I don't see the strain? He had you loosened up for a while there. I believe you were actually having the, you know, the *F* word? Fun?

"I can't figure it," Helen continued, scowling thoughtfully. "Ever since Thanksgiving, you're back to your old tricks. Working nights, working weekends. Working, working, working." She threw her hands in the air in exasperation. "Now I want to know what put the skids on the greatest romance since Julia Roberts fell for Richard Gere in *Pretty Woman*. Lord, I loved that movie," she added on a wistful sigh.

January smiled sadly. "Romance and movies mix, Helen, because you can edit out the rough parts. Real life doesn't come with guarantees of a carefully orchestrated plot."

"Bull pucky. Michael Hayward has happily-ever-after written all over him. Now what exactly is your problem?"

"I'm just being cautious, all right?"

"Cautious. Humph. You hang onto that word like a lifeline, and your ship isn't even sinking. The man loves you. He wants to marry you."

January couldn't meet Helen's eyes. "He thinks he wants to marry me. If he knew the whole truth he'd change his mind."

Too late, she realized what she'd just admitted. A quick glance at Helen confirmed it.

"Oh, Lord." Helen's hazel eyes, heavily shadowed with a dizzying shade of neon yellow, took on an iridescent quality as they narrowed at her. "You don't mean . . . Oh, January, sweetie, surely you've told him who you are. Oh, Lord," she repeated emphatically when she read the truth in January's eyes. "Oh, Lord, oh, Lord, oh, Lord."

Several moments of condemning silence followed before January rose from her desk and turned to stare out the window.

"I'm going to tell you something, girl," Helen said, "and I want you to listen and listen good."

Startled by the heated anger in Helen's voice, January turned to face her.

"For five years I have sat by and watched you sequester yourself from the rest of the world because you were too afraid, or too proud, to let anyone close enough to you to find out you are a vulnerable, hurtable person. But if you think that I'm going to stand back and watch you push away the only man who can wield a hammer big enough to break that protective barrier you have mortared around yourself, you've got another *think* coming."

"Helen," January began, "this is really none of your business."

"The hell it isn't, sweetie!" She rose from her

chair and advanced, one finger stabbing at the air between them. "You made it my business the day you hired me. I've watched you and learned from you and loved you like the child I never had the good fortune to have. I am entitled, dearheart. I am entitled to give you a piece of my mind if I feel like it. And I'm entitled to tell you that if you don't set things right with that man before sunset, you've not only lost the best thing to walk into your life since Toby, but you've lost yourself a secretary."

Stunned, January stared at her.

"I mean it, January. I can polish my nails at any desk in town. I don't have to sit behind that one and watch you walk through the rest of your life haunted by what you should have done and didn't do. I won't do it.

"Now you figure out some way to deal with this. And for God's sake, deal with it honestly. Start with asking yourself who you really think you're protecting by withholding your little secret. Yourself or Michael? And don't you dare hide behind that old argument that you're protecting your mother from a scandal. You know as well as I do that Michael would never do anything to hurt you or anyone you care about. Besides, Monica's a big girl and she can damn well take care of herself."

Knowing her eyes were shining with panic, January turned away.

Helen's hand on her arm stopped her. "The love of a good man is a precious, priceless gift, January," she said softly. "Just because you're afraid to accept it doesn't give you the right to throw it away."

Ten

Michael peeled away from the stoplight at full throttle, welcoming the bite of the early December wind as it whipped through his hair and stung his face. He welcomed, too, the explosion of adrenaline as the growling motorcycle beneath him skidded on a patch of ice and fishtailed dangerously before he set it right again. Since receiving Mac's phone call two hours ago, he'd have embraced hell itself if it would have taken his mind off the hollow gnawing ache eating at his gut.

But even the reverberating roar of the bike's powerful motor couldn't obliterate the memory of that call.

"Hayward! Hey, man, I can't believe I finally caught you at home. Lucky for you I'm persistent."

Recognizing the voice as that of his friend and contact in Denver, Michael had laughed into the receiver. "Last I knew, Mac, my answering machine was working just fine."

"I refuse to talk to those damn things. Besides, I knew you'd want to hear this first hand."

"I'm intrigued. What have you got?"

"Remember that Stewart woman you wanted me

to check on for you a few weeks ago? Well, I finally hit pay dirt, buddy. Hold onto your hat. You're not going to believe what I found out. . . ."

He'd absorbed Mac's news in numb silence. Then he'd spent the next two hours trying to outrun the truth. Or, at the very least, trying to outrun its implications. Only no matter how hard and fast he pushed his machine, Mac's news just kept catching up with him. It had chased him over miles of both I-25 and the Boulder Turnpike until finally, inevitably, it had driven him to the source.

His black rage had been diluted to weary acceptance by the time he pulled into January's drive. There was a light on inside. He stared at it for a long, brooding moment before he killed the motor, shoved down the kick stand, and walked up the path to her front door.

Even before Helen had delivered her speech that morning, January had known she was going to have to tell Michael. Even if it meant losing him, he deserved, no, he'd *earned* the right to know the truth from her. And she had lived the lie too long.

Praying she was prepared for the consequences, she'd waited until she got home from work, then with a tightness in her breast, picked up the phone to call him.

The roar of his cycle stopped her. She parted the curtain with a trembling hand, then watched through the window as he parked the bike and with a slow, almost reluctant determination walked to her front door.

Feeling a churning mixture of relief and the niggling sense of impending devastation, she opened the door.

As it always did, her heart leaped at the sight of him. There were so many faces of Michael. She would have welcomed any but the one standing in dangerous silence outside her door.

Neither the lover, the friend, nor the nurturing protector to a troubled little boy had come to her tonight. In black leather and faded denim, he was the dark knight of a dream-spun fairy tale, the ultimate road warrior who looked like he had just led the way out of hell.

He filled her doorway, his strong face reddened from the cold air, his dark hair wild and windblown. And his eyes—the beautiful blue eyes that turned to a warm yearning cobalt when he loved her, were as hard and unyielding as steel.

Confusion was the only thing that buffered her creeping fear, the dark sense of foreboding that inched across her skin and made her shiver.

"Michael," she said hesitantly when, tearing his gaze from hers, he pushed past her into the foyer. "I—I was just going to call you."

"Were you?" His voice was as stiff as the set of his shoulders.

He walked into the living room. Uncertain, she followed him to the doorway. When his restless gaze settled briefly on her, she nodded. "Yes, I was."

"Then I guess I saved you a call." He shoved his hands deep into the pockets of his leather jacket, glancing stonily around the room before his gaze returned to her face. "It's just as well. I think I've had about all the calls I can handle for one day anyway."

"Michael, what is it?" She'd never seen him this way, so cold and distant. And changed. "Has something happened?"

He searched her face with the hard, haunted eyes of a stranger.

"Yeah," he said finally. "I guess you could say something's happened."

The sharp foreshadowing of pain joined her sensation of dread. "Can you tell me?"

"It wasn't up to *me* to tell *you* anything, January. Or should I say Elaine?"

The room became so quiet that the creak of his supple leather jacket and his harsh, controlled breath sounded like explosions. She wanted, suddenly, to be anywhere but in this room. Folding her arms tightly around her waist, she sank into the nearest chair. "How," she asked, hearing the despair in her voice, "did you find out?"

"I'm a journalist. I have contacts," he answered sarcastically. "Since my kind can't be trusted with the truth, we pay people to dig up dirt for us. My God, January . . ." No longer capable of veiling his anger with indifference, he faced her with accusing eyes. "Was that the sum total of what you thought of me?"

Even knowing it was pointless, she couldn't stop herself. "I . . . was going to tell you." Pointless and pathetic.

He tipped his head back and snorted at the ceiling. "Right."

"Michael, listen to me. In the beginning, yes, I was frightened you might bring the whole thing to light again. I didn't know you then. I know you now."

"A hell of a difference that made, didn't it?"

"You matter to me now."

He stared right through her. "The only thing that matters is that I didn't find out from you. The only thing that matters," he restated with emphasis, "is that you didn't tell me."

"I didn't want to lose you."

"No, January," he corrected her coldly, "you didn't want to *trust* me."

The hurt in his voice tore at her and rekindled her own pain. "I didn't have any reason to trust you. Not in the beginning. And then . . ." She paused, realizing from his belligerent expression that he wouldn't listen to her argument. She reacted to his anger with her own. "Dammit, Michael, I didn't want anything from you! I tried to warn you. I didn't want any of this to happen."

He nodded grimly. "That, at least, is the truth. But then, you've always told me that much, haven't you? You told me, and I just wouldn't listen." He raked a hand through his hair. "Well, you finally got my attention. I hear you now, January, loud and clear. What you want is a safe unemotional, uncommitted life. What you don't want is to ever take a chance on something as frightening or as self-gratifying as love to threaten your peace of mind. And you want to sacrifice. Unless there's a sacrifice, it wouldn't fit into the profile of a martyr, would it? That much," he added bitterly, "has always been clear."

Wounded and wanting, she raised her eyes to his. "Michael, don't. I do love you."

He shook his head tiredly. "No. I finally realized you were right the first time. I think you might want to love me. You just don't want it enough to let go of your fear. I thought I could make it happen. I thought that if my love was strong enough, I could . . ." His voice trailed off, and he shrugged with weary acceptance. "Oh, hell. It doesn't matter what I thought because I was wrong. I was wrong and you were right. But hey, it wasn't a total loss. The sex was great, right?"

If he'd physically struck her, he couldn't have hurt her more.

Seeing that, he swore softly, succinctly. "Look, I'd better leave before I do a number on both of us. You said this wouldn't work. You said you couldn't give to this relationship. Well, you've finally convinced me that you can't."

He hunkered down in front of her, seemingly unmoved by the tears that were streaming down her cheeks. "It could have been so good, babe, if you had only let it. It could have been so good. But where there is no trust, there is no love."

He rose. Standing before her, he slowly zipped up his jacket and turned up the collar. "Take care, January. You just keep on taking care of everybody but you."

He touched a hand to her hair, then let it fall away, and without another word walked out the door.

January was no stranger to pain. She'd experienced it in more ways then she cared to remember—from the teeth-rattling crack of the back of her father's hand, to the aching shame of a child who blamed herself for not being loved, to the claw marks she'd earned in the occasional catfight in juvenile detention. But no memory, however vivid, no scar, however deep, hurt like the hollow, aching loneliness she felt when Michael left her.

Dusk had long since turned to darkness, loneliness had drifted aimlessly to despair before she rose from her chair. She walked through her dark empty house and laid down on her cold empty bed.

It was midnight before she realized what she had to do. Pride was precious little warmth to snuggle up to on a cold, black winter night. Love was a risk worth taking. Michael's love was worth any risk.

She'd been to his apartment a number of times, but she'd never arrived alone, and never in the dead of night. The dim hall lights provided little support for her already waning courage.

What if he wasn't home? What if he refused to see her? She wasn't the only one hurting. His grief was raw and real, his pride a victim too.

Using the key Michael had given her but that she'd never used, she quietly let herself into the apartment, then nearly fainted dead away when something cold and wet pressed against her leg. Suppressing a scream, she flattened her back against the door.

"George," she gasped, and dropped the hand that wasn't clutching her hammering chest to the dog's furry head. "You scared the life out of me."

George, oblivious to her trembling, nudged his cold nose into her palm. His tail thumped excitedly against the plush carpet.

She sank to the floor. Wrapping her arms around him, she buried her face against his thick coat. His solid friendly warmth gave her something to hang onto as she gathered her courage for the confrontation to come.

"If you've got any words of wisdom, George, I could sure use some help."

The dog whined and with a vigorous bump of his head begged her to scratch him behind his ears.

Fearing they'd wake up Michael before she was ready to face him, she shushed the exuberant dog. "That's a good idea," she whispered, giving him what he wanted, "but somehow, I don't think scratching Michael behind the ears is going to do the job. Got any other ideas?"

She jumped when a light clicked on and revealed a sullen, rumpled Michael sprawled in a chair by the sofa.

"You could start," he said, "by telling him what you're doing here at this hour of the night."

Startled and embarrassed that he'd been sitting there all this time in the dark, January rose slowly. She dragged a trembling hand through her hair.

Clutching her coat tightly around her, she advanced into the room on shaking legs.

"You took a foolish risk going out alone this time of night."

Though his face looked hardcast in darkness and shadows, his harsh voice held an encouraging amount of concern.

She drank in her fill of him sitting there in the dimly lit room. His shirt was unbuttoned and pulled from the waist of his jeans; his long legs were sprawled carelessly out in front of him; his gypsy black hair looked as if it had been raked repeatedly with long, punishing fingers. He was so beautifully male, so obviously hurting, she had to fight to keep from throwing herself into his arms.

"Sometimes," she whispered, meeting his tired eyes, "some risks are worth taking."

He dragged a hand over his face. "Why now, January? Why tonight?"

"Because I love you and because until tonight I didn't know I couldn't bear to live my life without you." Her confession came out fast and sure.

He was quiet for a long, tense moment, and she wondered if she was too late. At last he said, "If this admission has conditions attached to it—"

"No conditions, Michael." Not letting herself think about it, she knelt quickly between his legs. Because she couldn't not touch him, she placed a shaking hand on each knee. "Please . . . please just listen."

He swallowed hard, then dropped his head back against the chair's plump cushion.

With a tight knot of anxiety squeezing her chest, she began without hesitation. "From the time I can remember, when my father used to come home from work every night, it was always after he'd made his nightly rounds of the bars.

"Some nights," she continued softly when Michael

looked at her with surprise, "he'd come home happy. He'd sing and dance and whirl my mother around in a circle, then he'd pat me on the head and tell me what a good little girl I was. But most nights . . ." She paused and licked her suddenly dry lips. "Most nights, he'd come home angry. Those were the nights my mother used to make me go to my room and lock the door. I'd lie on my bed and cover my head with a pillow. Then I'd sing so I couldn't hear if he was hitting her."

Michael's hand fell heavily to her hair. In the pale light she saw him swallow.

"Sometimes I'd try to help her. But sometimes I'd just run away because I knew that when he was finished with her, he'd turn on me. And then I'd feel so guilty."

"January, don't—"

"Michael," she implored, "I'm not telling you this to make you feel sorry for me. I'm telling you so you'll understand. I always thought the reason my father hurt me was because I had done something to deserve it. After all, the people in your family are supposed to love you. They're supposed to protect you, not hurt you. Yet he did. Often.

"I could never understand what I'd done wrong. So my mind—like the minds of most children in abusive situations—helped me handle those confusing feelings. It repressed the things I couldn't handle. It trained me to block, to deny, to say 'this isn't happening to me.'

"What you need to understand," she said, meeting his tortured gaze, "is that after years of repressing feelings and facts that were just too hard to deal with, it's still not an easy thing for me to accept the truth about what happened to me. I still feel the shame even though I know it wasn't my fault."

"The shame was his," Michael said gruffly.

"Yes," she agreed, "it was. But sometimes I still have trouble accepting that. In my head, I know. But in my heart . . ." She took his hand and placed it over her breast where her heart beat rapidly. "In my heart, the child in me still wonders why he didn't love me.

"Michael, when you came back into my life after all those years, you unleashed feelings inside me that I didn't want to deal with. You scared me half out of my mind. I just wanted you to go away. When you wouldn't, I wanted to hate you. Not only did you make hating you impossible, you made me want to love you. You made me want to be loved. I didn't think I could let that happen. I didn't think I could handle the responsibility of being loved.

"So I panicked all over again. And then— Then you asked the impossible. You wanted my trust, something I'd never given to anyone."

She lifted his hand to her cheek. "But when you walked out that door tonight and I thought I'd never see you again, I realized I would risk everything—the shame, the memories, even my mother's future—if I could only have you back."

With a groan that relayed anger, frustration, and a wealth of unbridled love, he hauled her off the floor and onto his lap. "You never lost me, babe. You couldn't be so lucky. I just needed some pout time, some poor me time. Come morning, I was going to be hammering at your door like a big strong wind."

He wrapped her tightly in his arms and sought her mouth with his, kissing her tenderly, reverently.

She returned the kiss without restraint, pouring into it the love, the fear of loss, and the heart-mending sense of relief she was feeling. Then she gently pushed herself away. "Michael, there's more—"

"I know everything I need to know," he said, pulling her back against him.

She shook her head firmly. "You need to know that I trust you. I need to *know* that you know."

He brushed the hair back from her face. "I do, love."

"Michael, I need to tell you the truth about my father's death."

He met her eyes. "It was a long time ago, January. Maybe it's best forgotten."

"I didn't kill him," she blurted out before he stopped her.

He stared at her, silent, considering.

"I didn't kill him," she repeated, not waiting for his reaction. "My mother was very weak, physically and mentally, by that time. She'd given up. Or at least I thought she had. The night it happened, I was sick in bed with the flu. He came home wanting his dinner, and when it wasn't ready because Mother had been taking care of me, he came after me."

The memory made her pulse accelerate, her breathing grow quick and shallow. "I was too sick to get away from him. Something—something snapped inside my mother. She took his gun from his bureau drawer and begged him to stop hitting me. When he wouldn't, she shot him."

She was distantly aware of Michael gathering her closer, of his strong hand running soothingly along the length of her hip. "I remember thinking, if they find out, they'll take her away. I didn't want to be all alone. She was my mother and I didn't want them to take her."

A tear fell down her cheek and onto the soft cotton of his shirt.

"She didn't remember what she'd done. It was easy to convince her and the court that it was me. They would have prosecuted her—"

"But not a thirteen-year-old child who had acted in self-defense," Michael finished for her. "My brave little heroine. You've had lots of practice saving souls, haven't you?"

"I've had lots of practice hiding behind that lie and so many others. I don't want to hide anything from you any longer."

He hugged her hard, then rising to his feet, settled her in his chair. "There's something I want to show you," he said, and disappeared into his office.

When he came out, he was carrying several dog-eared, typewritten sheets of paper.

She looked from it to him questioningly. "I don't understand."

"It's a piece I wrote but never took to print. Read the date under the by-line."

She did. "Michael, you wrote this fifteen years ago."

"Read the article. All of it. I'll make us some coffee."

When Michael returned to the living room, she was staring at the last page of the article. Her head came up when he settled a hip on the arm of the chair.

"You knew," she said, looking from the pages in her lap to him. "All these years, you knew."

She waved away the mug of coffee.

"Michael . . . how?"

"I'm not very proud of how. The fact of the matter is, I caught your mother offguard one day when I paid her an unannounced visit. She was distraught, and like you said, broken. She told me everything."

Her eyes, when they met his, were full of love. "But you didn't print it."

"No, I didn't print it. Even back then you got to me." He shook his head. "You were thirteen years old, a sad and sorry thirteen, and something about you, a proud and angry courage, a promise of something special, made me feel things and think about things that had nothing to do with good copy or an exclusive. I just couldn't hurt you any more than you'd already been hurt."

No gift he could have given her could have touched her more. It was a gift of insight into the heart of the special man he was. "I love you," she said simply, eloquently.

"Yes," he agreed, "you do."

The uncategorical trust shining in her eyes told him she was ready to make the ultimate commitment.

He responded to that look with a slow, intimate kiss. "Why don't we forget the coffee," he murmured, "and I'll demonstrate how the luckiest man in the world shows his woman exactly how much he loves her."

Epilogue

Working at her desk in her new office in Griffin House, January still couldn't believe that her most secret dream was now reality. It was a dream that the woman, January Stewart, had held close to her heart. A dream she hadn't dared to share with anyone for fear that by telling, she would somehow destroy its chances of fruition, and then children like Elaine January Griffin would never find the help they needed.

Now, though, she shared everything with Michael. And one late, lovely midnight, lazy from spent passion and bathed in the glow of his love, she'd told him her most secret dream. Because of Michael, that dream was now cemented into fact.

Rubbing a crick out of her neck, she rose from her desk and peered out the still-uncurtained window. The tree-lined street was quiet and peaceful, and the promising scent of the warm April morning drifting through the open window dispelled some of the paint and varnish odors that hung heavily in the old house.

The scene outside never failed to make her smile. If she had painted a picture of the neighborhood she'd envisioned for Griffin House, it would have mirrored what met her eyes.

The curbs were lined with oaks, the lawns fertile and green. Here and there the deeper green of crocus and jonquils poked bravely through the spring-warmed earth, and from the corner of her eyes she caught the red, white, and blue flutter of a flag waving in the breeze. It was a neighborhood made for children. And this old Victorian house would soon be full of children. Bruised children. Battered children. Children in need of a little love, a little hope, and a place where they could just hang out and be kids.

She opened the window wider, then smiled as she heard the distant purr of Michael's bike grow into a loud roar. He and Toby cruised up the street and came to a rumbling stop at the curb.

Hanging back in her doorway, she watched as Michael, with an exuberant, red-cheeked Toby on his heels, bounded through the huge front door.

The spacious airy foyer doubled as an informal reception area and Helen's work station. Both Michael and Toby stopped dead in their tracks when they got a load of Helen and her outfit.

"Hot mama!" Toby said, fanning a hand in the air.

January grinned from her office doorway as Michael, executing a leering doubletake, joined in on the outrageous flirting. "Has Leonard seen you in that outfit yet?"

Smiling like the cat who swallowed the canary and looking like the canary who escaped the cat in a yellow Lycra jumpsuit and street-sign green fringed scarf draped around her neck, Helen turned a quick pirouette. "Think his heart can take it?"

"If it can't, you know who to call."

"Humph. It won't be you, big talker."

Wounded, Michael slumped against the wall, his hand flattened theatrically against his chest.

"I've got your number, Hayward," Helen grumbled good-naturedly. "You're a one woman man, and I'm not the woman. Besides, you're not nearly as cute without your diamond earring."

"That diamond's fine right where it is, thank you very much," January said, flashing her diamond and ruby engagement ring with a panache that earned a thumbs-up from Helen.

Smiling as January joined their little group, Michael pulled her against his side. "Hey, babe. How's it going?"

January loved the look that came over his face as he bent to kiss her. It was the look that said, "I love you," the look that had talked her into accepting his ring and setting a wedding date. And it was the look that had made her laugh and then cry when he'd presented her with the deed to this house, along with a promise from the zoning commission that there would be no problem establishing a group home.

"Come on, Toby," Helen said tactfully. "Let's get out of here . . . unless you want to watch."

Toby made a sour face.

"I tried out the new oven this morning," Helen went on. "By the time we polish off some of those cookies I baked, they ought to have this mushy stuff out of their system."

"Don't bet on it," Michael murmured, pulling January fully into his arms. "And don't let her kid you, Toby. She likes this mushy stuff as much as I do."

He ruffled Toby's hair as the boy breezed by, making his great escape.

"Hello," Michael drawled, settling January against his hips. "And look out. Now that I've got you alone, I intend to have my way with you."

"Hi, yourself," she said as she looped her arms around his neck. "You can have me any way you want me, but your imagination's much more active than mine if you call being surrounded by a garrison of electricians, carpenters, and assorted painters who are apt to pop into the room at any moment, having me alone."

"You always have to be so damn practical," he muttered, then kissed her sweetly.

"Have I told you lately that I love you?" she asked, brushing his impossibly too-long hair away from his face.

He kissed her again. "Sounds like a great song title."

She smiled against his mouth. "Have I told you lately how much I appreciate that you've made Griffin House possible?"

"You can appreciate the devil out of me when you get me home alone tonight."

"It's a date," she assured him, and then, arms linked loosely around each other's waists, they wandered through the house, delighting in the work in progress.

Not only had Michael put up the money for the purchase of Griffin House, he'd footed the bill for the extensive remodeling required to bring the six-bedroom facility up to code. And he'd tirelessly devoted time and voice to fund raising, insuring the operation of Boulder's newest shelter for battered children for at least the next five years.

Since January could provide her clients better access to her services there, it had only made sense to relocate her office to Griffin House. Now that she was settled in, all that remained were the finishing touches to the house itself.

The contractor assured her that all would be ready when the full staff, including house parents and counselors, arrived the first of May. It couldn't come soon enough for January, as Human Services had already given them enough referrals to fill all six bedrooms.

The only shadow to darken her horizon was the reality that a waiting list existed. Many more children than Griffin House could accommodate were in need of a safe house, a home where they could receive the love and attention they needed to help set them on the right path. That knowledge still hurt her.

"Hey . . ." Michael must have read her thoughts through her eyes. "You can't do it all at once, Counselor."

"I know." She gave him a quick smile and brightened, looking around her. "This place . . . it's beautiful, isn't it? It's like the house I always imagined growing up in. The open staircase, the shining hardwood floors, the leaded glass windows—" She caught herself and stopped abruptly. "And it's going to be so full of love. Isn't it wonderful?"

"You're wonderful," he said, pulling her back into his arms.

"Hey, Michael, January," Toby called from the open kitchen door. "You *gotta* try these cookies. They're like, awesome."

"Be right there, sport."

"Amazing," January murmured, "what a cookie and a little love can do for a kid."

"If only *you* were that easy," Michael teased, draping an arm around her shoulders and walking with her toward the kitchen.

"You really love him, don't you?"

"Just like you do."

She thought of the way Toby had blossomed right before her eyes into a carefree, loving child. As soon as the paper work was complete, he would legally belong to them. "Loving that child is easy."

Michael nodded. "And less complex than loving a woman. But loving a woman"—his eyes glittered warmly as he fitted her snugly against his side—"loving *my* woman is infinitely more fun."

Later that night, he showed her just how much fun.

THE EDITOR'S CORNER

As winter's chilly blasts bring a rosy hue to your cheeks and remind you of the approaching holiday season, why not curl up in a cozy blanket with LOVESWEPT's own gift bag of six heartwarming romances.

The ever-popular Helen Mittermeyer leads the list with **KRYSTAL,** LOVESWEPT #516. Krystal Wynter came to Seattle to start over in a town where no one could link her with the scandalous headlines that had shattered her life. But tall, dark, and persistent Cullen Dempsey invades her privacy, claiming her with an intoxicating abandon that awakens old fears and ensnaring her in a web of desire that keeps her from running away. A moving, sensual romance—and another winner from Helen Mittermeyer!

LOVESWEPT's reputation for innovation continues as Terry Lawrence takes you right up to the stars with **EVER SINCE ADAM**, #517, set in an orbiting station in outer space! Maggie Mullins is there to observe maverick astronaut Adam Strade in the environment she helped design—not to succumb to his delicious flirting. And while Adam sweeps her off her feet in zero gravity, he fights letting her get close enough to discover his hidden pain. Don't miss this unique love story. Bravo, Terry, for a romance that's out of this world!

Please give a rousing welcome to Patricia Potter and her first LOVESWEPT, **THE GREATEST GIFT,** #518. Patricia has already garnered popular and critical success with her numerous historical romances, and in **THE GREATEST GIFT** she proves her flair with short, contemporary romance, as well. Writing about a small-town teacher isn't reporter Lane Drury's idea of a dream assignment—until she meets David Farrar. This charming rogue soon convinces her she's captured the most exciting job of all in a romance that will surely be a "keeper." Look for more wonderful stories from Patricia Potter in the year to come.

Let Joan J. Domning engulf you with a wave of passion in **STORMY'S MAN,** LOVESWEPT #519. Gayle Stromm certainly feels as if she's in over her head with Cass Starbaugh, who's six feet six inches of hard muscles, bronzed skin, and sun-streaked hair. Gayle's on vacation to escape nightmares, but caring for the injured mountain climber only makes her dream of a love she thinks she can never have. Cass can't turn down a challenge, though, and he'd do anything to prove to Stormy that she's all the woman he wants. An utterly spellbinding romance by the incomparable Joan J. Domning.

Marvelously talented Maris Soule joins our fold with the stirring **JARED'S LADY,** LOVESWEPT #520. Maris already has several romances to her credit, and you'll soon see why we're absolutely thrilled to have her. Jared North can't believe that petite Laurie Crawford is the ace tracker the police sent to find his missing niece, and, to Laurie's dismay, he insists on joining the search. She's had enough of overprotective men to last a lifetime, yet raw hunger sparks inside her at his touch. Together these two create an elemental force that will leave you breathless and looking for the next LOVESWEPT by Maris Soule.

IRRESISTIBLE, LOVESWEPT #521 by beloved author Joan Elliot Pickart, is the perfect description for Pierce Anderson. This drop-dead-gorgeous architect thinks he's hallucinating when a woman-sized chicken begs him to unzip her. But when a dream girl emerges from the feathers, he knows the fever he feels has nothing to do with the flu! Calico Smith struggles to resist the sensual power of Pierce's kissable lips. She's worked so hard for everything she has, while he's never fought for what he wanted—until now. Another fabulous romance from Joan Elliott Pickart.

And (as if these six books aren't enough) LOVESWEPT is celebrating the joyous ritual of weddings with a contest for you, a contest that will have three winners! Look for details in the January 1992 LOVESWEPTS.

Don't forget FANFARE, where you can expect three superb books this month. **THE FLAMES OF VENGEANCE** is the second book in bestselling Beverly Byrne's powerful trilogy. From rebellion plotted beneath cold, starry skies to the dark magic that stalks the sultry Caribbean night, Lila Curran's web, baited with lust and passion, is carefully being spun. Award-winning Francine Rivers delivers a compelling historical romance in **REDEEMING LOVE**. Sold into sin as a child, beautiful, tormented "Angel" never believed in love until the strong and tender Michael Hosea walked into her life. Can their radiant happiness conquer the darkest demons from her past? Much-acclaimed Sandra Brown will find a place in your heart—if she hasn't already—with **22 INDIGO PLACE**. Rebel millionaire James Paden has a dream—to claim 22 Indigo Place and its alluring owner, Laura Nolan, the rich man's daughter for whom he'd never been good enough. Three terrific books from FANFARE, where you'll find only the best in women's fiction.

As always at this season, we send you the same wishes. May your New Year be filled with all the best things in life—the company of good friends and family, peace and prosperity, and, of course, love.

Warm wishes from all of us at LOVESWEPT and FANFARE,

Nita Taublib

Nita Taublib
Associate Publisher, LOVESWEPT
Publishing Associate, FANFARE